W9-CMN-823

✴ *LILO'S DIARY*

BOOKS BY RICHARD M. ELMAN

Lilo's Diary ✳

By RICHARD M. ELMAN

Charles Scribner's Sons · New York

A-7.68 [H]

Printed in the United States of America
Library of Congress Catalog Card Number 68-27791

For Elie Wiesel
For Emily
For M. S.

An appalling and horrible thing
is come to pass in the land:
the prophets prophesy in the service of falsehood,
and the priests bear rule at their beck;
and my people love to have it so;
what then will ye do in the end thereof?

JEREMIAH

✳ *LILO'S DIARY*

Lilo: 1944

That I am beautiful it cannot be denied. My face. My eyes. My hair. Surely, few are endowed as fortunately as I have been. How it bores me! Alex stares and stares, as if he could discover some meaning in my loveliness, a reason—there are no reasons. To be beautiful is my fate.

How vain and how boring to be so vain! When I was a child I honestly believed myself to be ill-favored. Perhaps I was much happier then, for there was something that I had not yet attained: This face. These eyes. This hair. My figure. I wanted so much to be beautiful and it was to be my fate. Now what is left? A stares as if he would make me ugly again by the act of contemplation. But he can do no such thing. I am exactly the thing I am, and there is no turning away from it.

If there were some chance that I might become ill-favored it would profit me to describe the way I am now so that posterity would have the record of my transactions with the physical world. Nothing is ever going to change for me, not even through my death. Why then describe? Because there is so little else I can do. We live here as prisoners, each imprisoned within himself, each a victim of his own crass appetites and vanities, and one must gaze into a looking glass to see a stranger. So I have been gazing (and next door, or downstairs perhaps, others are similarly occupied) and what I see disturbs me by its very perfection: I am beautiful, and I am cold. No doubt that is why A stares at me as he does.

Let this mirror record, consequently, that the writer is a twenty-one-year-old woman of mixed Jewish-Hungarian descent, engaged in marriage to the son of her uncle by marriage,

Newman Yagodah, the advocate and factor, and not terribly discontented withal. Her life has been an instruction in humility: despite the late blossoming of her beauty, she has never humbled herself before the expectation of ecstasy or passion or delight. . . .

Lise Lotte Gero, for so she was called, is a girl of independent means which are all presently under the guardianship of her future father-in-law. She lives with her maiden aunt, Pepi, and her two girl cousins, and with A. If her smile invites him, her innermost feelings repel. To be the captive of such a smile is not alone the fate of her various victims, but of the girl herself. Her smile is something pasted onto her face, stiff, involuntary and painful, just as her hair is as blonde and stitched on as doll's hair and her eyes as blue as Bristol glass. Fräulein Gero's is an animated doll's face, in sum, a face of very special contrivance, able to simulate the warmth of flesh itself, so that even she is sometimes confused . . . I mean, she feels confused . . . and her body is lean and silken, dusty with sensations, so that she will sometimes find herself absently running the tips of her fingers lightly across that flesh—Ah, what lovely agony. . . . Abandoned to revery, which is the greatest of all passions, she, being without feelings, is never quite the victim of even such lusts. That fate she reserves for others. . . .

Alex, for example, who is to be her husband, and already would seem to enjoy all of the privileges of the married state. Fräulein Gero tells herself she does what she does because the times have made her lax, whereas the truth is she does not feel what she does; it is always happening elsewhere, as it were, and to somebody else. The simplest thing, then, is not to resist, let it happen to the other, for then it will go away. That is what she tells herself and that is what she does . . . and that is why she has these victims.

The son of Newman Yagodah is not an attractive lover. Neither is he considerate or, for that matter, affectionate in his love-making. Again she tells herself the times have made him greedy, whereas the truth is even she can see he suffers because of the way he stares and wants her. A stares endlessly, as if hurt beyond repair. Hasn't he, she wonders, any looking glasses in his rooms?

Doch, these reflections in English rapidly become pretentious, and, if they are not occasioned by the general conflagration or the particularly awful fate one imagines to be in prospect for the bourgeois clan Yagodah-Gero, they are the consequences of certain very specific historical circumstances having to do with the fact that our grandfather was a lecher, our parents cold and greedy takers, and that I was once plain and am now beautiful. Is it possible that A is so incredulous of my beauty even when we are together? He stares and stares, as if he expected me to reproduce myself as plain to match his own ungainliness. That cannot be my fate. I know what he must think—that he will lose me. *Where would I go? Who will take me in?* Odd, to be beautiful and yet so unwanted. Despite myself, I have succeeded in keeping the world at bay. My feelings give me a fictitious ugliness. There is no doubt that I am forbidding, like the coldest marble. You may embrace a statue in its nakedness but you cannot have it. No, never. Forever it will remain cold and hard to the touch long after your hands have fled and your feelings have passed. *Is that to be my fate? Is this the way I am?*

Today, in the attic, I read some love letters from the late Imre Geiyer, our granduncle, to his first wife. Like all Hungarian women of Jewish ancestry, it was her destiny—*her destiny?*—to be a whore, as cold to the act as if it were happening to another person. A brooch mounted with her cameo was among the papers. Plain to see she was a very handsome person.

"You will never know," the poor Imre wrote her, "the extent of my suffering because it is not the manner of your suffering. I wish to possess and am repelled in the very act of possessing, but you suffer because you wish nothing of me or of any man . . . only to exist in the perfectly calm solitude of your loveliness, to be adored and to cause men to feel the guilt of their adoration."

Pauvre petit Imre! I pity him and all men, all, that is, except Uncle Newman, for he is not like a man but an abacus, a calculating machine, hardly even human enough to feel. Is that why he frightens me so? Because I know I cannot enslave him? How dreadfully vain I have become. While the world groans and sacrifices itself to the god of war, I stare into my pier glass talking schoolgirl nonsense.

What else can one do? We are prisoners here. I feel it. The other girls feel it. Even Alex, I am sure, feels it, although, thus far, we have not dared to speak of it at all. He is my lover and my intended, but there are many things we do not speak about. Is that what Granduncle Imre meant when he spoke of the inequality of suffering? Granduncle Imre was no fool, an idolator of women, who suffered deservingly, yes, but not a fool, whereas A takes and then suffers upon discovering that he has grabbed with both arms for a stone.

"You allow me every liberty," Uncle Imre wrote: "Was that to deny me yourself?"

Afterwards, I happened to glance through the attic window toward the square. The usual scene: Soldiers, soldiers, always soldiers, and empty carts with bedraggled and shopworn goods, and a few of the usual crowd of Clig loafers. You might say I was staring at nothing . . . nothing at all . . . except that it presently seemed as if that nothingness was staring back at me. By the purest accident, my aimless wayward glance had joined with that of another: a pair of glass-blue eyes, blonde hair, a smile that seemed to be forming words, cruel words, obscene words, but I was, oddly enough, amused.

Dienst being *dienst* and *schnaps* being *schnaps*, as Uncle Newman likes to put it, why should it matter that his old friend Skirzeny's eldest should have been asking me with signs and lip movements to meet him after dark behind the gate of the big house? Well-instructed in the niceties of the new curfew laws, I had no intention of doing any such thing, so I stared and smiled back, with a rising feeling of blood racing throughout my smallest veins, neither encouraging or discouraging M in his brutishness, a picture which, if he dared to act as if he had been encouraged by it to take liberties, would be sure to protest that she was just a picture, neutral, self-absorbed, unthinking . . . mere pigment. . . .

Magda's daughter has been seen walking the streets. Strange how it is with them. That which we say we would never do (and would not if we could possibly help it) *they* take to naturally. Would I *ever* be reduced to that? Never! Not even if it should cost me my life. Though what I am doing is hardly that much more respectable.

It is, however, a fact that I alone know of what I am about. A and me, I mean. Whereas with Magda and her daughter all Clig talks— that she goes with soldiers, that she has had a child by one of them, or is expecting a child, I don't know which. . . .

And Magda and her husband are poor simple folk. So religious too. Their religion! They are all whores or panderers! To A, Magda was a second mother, a gentle friend when all the Yagodah children were young. Does she worry about her own children? It seems not. It seems they are *fated* to be as they are. Today she comes to visit (it is her way of still helping

Aunt Ilona with the housework for money without causing malicious gossip, for *they do* need the extra money it appears, despite his promotion) and, when she sees me, she comes up to me and embraces me, pressing me to her so hard that I can feel the outlines of the silver cross against my bosoms.

Fancy! She wears a silver cross, is always buying candles, cheap religious pictures, the figures of saints in porcelain for their cottage, and yet she is the mother of a whore, and there are still two younger daughters. If this war goes on much longer, they will also be taking to the streets. As Uncle Newman says: "It is beginning to hurt the working man, this war. . . ."

Not far from here is the town of Szemoszekelyvar, a royal free town settled by Armenians who have long since become "Magyarized." It is the seat of the Greek Catholic bishop, a small place with peaked roofs, mineral springs, a salt works. At the north end of the town is a castle erected in 1540, and there are the remains of a Roman fortress a half kilometre or so farther along the banks of the river. Before the war, my late father had many dealings in Szemosze-kelyvar. We summered there in a woods cross-river from the castle. These woods were the scene of a great battle some one hundred years ago between the forces of Count Petofi and the Russian Voivodes. Occasionally, when we would wander together to pick the little white or yellow stemmed mushrooms that grew there, the bones of some long-dead hussar would poke up through the rich dark loam of the soil. Our childhood playground was a boneyard, and the castle had long since become a prison.

All castles are prisons in fine. As true of Uncle Newman's estate as of the old stone patrimony of the Counts Borba. . . .

But why do I say such things?

Do I know what I am saying?

How awful I am!

It is wretched to be so spiteful.

Am I bored with myself? Then I must learn the virtues of polite hypocrisy.

Am I unhappy? Then I must lie with a good face.

But I am wretched and spiteful and it is a bore, and yet it is also my sole delight. Being miserable, makes me happy. Or so the contemplation of myself would seem to indicate.

Bright sun this morning, then a fogginess which seems to have settled over the whole household. Over second breakfast I count the stitches on the lace table cloth and ask myself what kind of person goes to so much trouble . . . This reflection is occasioned by an incident which takes place.

Uncle Newman had been up early, seeing to his accounts. He came into the room where the buffet was spread, as frowzy as a distempered bear, and then proceeded to lecture me: "Your parents were prodigious fools; not a single one of their investments has proved out; I am thinking that it may be necessary to redeem all your holdings as cash if you are to be left with anything . . . *anything at all.*"

If I was cranky because of the early hour, there might have been some excuse for what I said, but I had already bathed and walked in the garden and I felt, in truth, rather light-headed.

"It isn't necessary for you to be so solemn," I declared. "We all know you are a sly old fellow. So why not do it? Simply go to it, Uncle. . . ."

Although the elder Yagodah pretended to go along with my joke, I could tell that he felt pricked. He mumbled something to himself about irresponsibility and was shortly leaving for his study once again.

Cousin Alex, who was also present, then added as I got up to carry away my dishes from the table: "Father hasn't been feeling very well. We should try not to upset him even in jest. . . ."

What else could my dear cousin say? I had attacked his father. That he was my fiancé should have meant nothing to him. I had insulted the man whom every precept of Jewish life taught him to love and honor. I was in the wrong.

How boring it is to be always in the wrong, even to think of oneself in that way. It is almost as boring as being dependent on these people. Yes, that is what we are, Aunt Pepi and myself, like dependent spinsters, whether we care to be or not. It is entirely wretched and boring, but it is surely not Uncle Newman's fault.

My uncle took me into his house and has treated me, in a time of great uncertainty, as one of his family. If that means that he must belabor me as a father, it is only to be expected. And if he *is* cheating me of my inheritance, is it not his due in return for the charity he has shown to me? No, I suspect the truth is that I am not used to living in a family, for he is as kind to me as he is toward his own children about things like rations and work deferments, or, at least, he tries to be. But I have lived away from family life for too long.

In school we knew the rules and never had

to bother with other people's feelings. Those in charge of us in the Swiss school were paid not to have feelings. They were always correct and could not be hurt. When my mother died and I had to return here, it might have been better to live alone. Where and how? Would I have been so well-protected? That Schlesinger girl, who also was an orphan, was taken away with the first labor drafts in 1942. They said she would only be working in a factory. I doubt very much if she is still alive. . . .

So, if I was not prepared to fend completely for myself, dare I have the right to expect not to be humiliated? I owe my Uncle Newman a great deal, if the truth were to be told, my life, among so many other things, and perhaps it is out of gratitude toward him that I allow myself to do these things with his son. . . .

What a terrible thought! That the father's favors procure for the son . . . I am to marry Alex. He must never see what I am writing here. He must never know.

As for the other, our putative relation M.S.,

with his insolent stare and chronically insolvent father, let him think whatever he likes. I feel nothing for him. If I can smile so openly it is because it would be an effort to discourage him. It might even require feeling something perhaps . . .

In any event, I am committed to marrying Alex and to allowing him to possess me . . .

My old nurse has shown up here at the household with souvenirs of the family: a photograph, my school leaving dress, Father's Diary of Living Thoughts, my mother's sewing basket. Nurse is a good old crone, not really like the others, but I cannot bring myself to talk to her about those times. I offer her tea in the kitchen and send her on her way, promising to visit, an impossibility, as we both well know.

I am busy all day copying lists on the typewriter for Aunt Yagodah. An inventory of the household things:

chairs
tables
lamps
coverlets

1 small secretary with inlaid leather top and claw feet (very old)

1 large chaise (suitable for lying-in purposes) with white muslin upholstery and pillows

a large seven-branched candelabra in brass

½ dozen small candlesticks in worked silver

a silver kiddush cup (large) with brass tracery etched in a *fleur de lis* pattern

the same with ram's horns and harps

a silver salver with six-pointed stars

the same in German silver

a green glass pickle jar (very old)

200 pieces Rosenthal with settings for 13 and assorted serving pieces

50 assorted glass wine and water goblets (variously tinted)

1 crystal dinner bell

3 large Dunkle silver serving spoons with crests

18 tomato plates

4 decanters (Bohemian crystal)

1 Reissenweber water pitcher in the blue rose pattern.

How the list goes on and on.

We haven't even gotten to the chintz room.

There must be two pages reserved for book ends and ashtrays alone.

tea sets

napkin rings

chocolate cups and a pitcher

Sachettes Douvées and a very special eiderdown

Grandmother's feather boas

a Bible bound in silver

Everything, it seems, must be listed and enumerated. And just what is the purpose?

I am annoyed that my parents' things are to be included. They are, after all, my only substantial legacy and came here in crates still unbroken.

If I were a different person I would argue about this matter, but it is not so nice to risk the threat and accusation of ingratitude.

And the list does go on and on. I merely am asked to transcribe on the typewriter from Aunt Ilona's tiny crabbed script, that queer by-product of her queer education; and so I do not complain but continue transcribing:

3 Wasserstrom chairs (very good)
a large copper basin
10 enamel platters
14 beaten silver punch cups
1 japanned platter with citrons and bees and pomegranates
1 curling iron
1 steam iron
1 GDF iron
1 flat iron
1 cuffing iron
1 black iron
3 clothing dummies (Perl, Sarah & Ilona)

41 assorted knitting and embroidering needles
1 Groiner-Taube "luft" iron
1 Zimmerman consolette

And in the bathroom closet off the downstairs sitting room:

8 apothecary-style dispensers
4 blackberry bowls
1 spider glass fruit compote
1 silver pier glass in the grapevine design

And we are only listing those things which we still use. If we were observing the dietary laws seven other closets might be suddenly opened up for this inventory. In the meantime Aunt Ilona occasionally fondles some item that is especially precious or dear to her, observes my admiration of it, and announces: "This will be yours someday." But there is so very little that I really and truly like. I try to be nice and to seem interested, but I am not such a very good actress.

Tonight we are planning to inventory the chambers on the upper floors.

A bad scene. My aunt has shown me her wedding picture: the two of them looking stiff and stupid and coarse, all done up in a heavy silver frame, the lust popping out on their faces. For twenty years she has kept it in her bureau.

Today she says: "I want you and Alex to have this someday."

I don't know what to say, certainly not "thank you."

"It is up to Alex, of course," I begin.

But she starts to weep and runs off into the other room.

✳

From Division Number 9 of the Department of Defense came a letter today for our near neighbors, the Frankenauers. Their only son, Gyorg, has died of influenza, at work somewhere in Austria. Since our cousin Laszlo Stark was on the same "consignment," we are blackened by the news, *all of us*. Rumors of every kind now exist: Of huge camps where the dead are thrown into cauldrons of lye to make fat while the dying work until they have no more strength . . .

Terrible rumors! Of fusillades, mass executions, epidemics. They are so awful that they are hard to believe, and so they must be true. If only the war news were somewhat more optimistic, but it is so confusing . . . We hear of defections among the Rumanians and of massive German reprisals and counterattacks. None of us seems to have any hope except, perhaps, Uncle Newman. If he knows as much as we think we know, he is a very great actor and even courageous. My uncle insists that Germany must soon come to terms with this man Roosevelt now that she can no longer sustain her war aims and that an alliance will be formed against the Bolsheviks . . .

Meanwhile, he points out, our best interests are served by keeping strictly to ourselves . . .

If only I knew more about so many things it would be possible for me to argue. How, when I am almost totally in ignorance of

politics? We are as fated to my uncle's interpretations of events as we are to my beautiful
face. Yesterday, at the market I was approached
by a certain dark woman who has stared at me
before upon occasion. She wears mourner's
clothes and always smells strongly of jasmine
scent. Could I help staring back? She, of course,
seemed to be willing me to do exactly that. At
last, when I had completed my purchases, I
began to walk away. "Not so fast, Miss . . .

"You seem to have left this behind."

The paper the woman handed me was a
Communist leaflet: "The coming struggle in
Hungary emerges . . ." I did not throw the
thing away, as I should have, but buried it in
the pocket of my skirt and hurried along home
again.

At the breakfast table this morning a
strange experience. Uncle Newman was reading
a letter aloud from the caretaker of Kishavas
. . . a stumbling piece about crops failing and
encroaching farms, demanding intercession
from, of all people, Uncle Newman, when I felt
my "courses" coming on. Fleeing the table, I
discovered that I was mistaken.

It has happened again at lunch and again I was mistaken.

I wish I understood what was happening inside my body.

Question: Who is Adam Geiger?

Answer: He is the ghost of a pale little boy with a sweet face and a stammer with whom I played when I was not quite three years old. His father killed him first and now my future sister-in-law Perl hopes to exhume the corpse. So that she may have the pleasure of killing him once again . . .

Poor weak little Adam. When he tries to seem saintly he is merely absurd. Today he asks, with nothing more in mind, I am sure, than the asking: "Wouldn't it be nice if the whole family, yours and ours, could break the fast together after the Days of Awe?"

Perl: "If we are lucky enough to even fast . . ."

Uncle Newman: "We shall not make plans. We shall not make foolish gloomy statements either, for that matter."

Perl (again): "Tedious old man . . ."

Adam: "Dearest heart, your father means no insults . . ."

Perl (again): "Dearest heart! Adam, you sound like a sentimental gramaphone record."

Alex and I are very amused, of course, and so she turns against us: "Do you see how they are mocking us, Adam? And you would have me ask your parents to invite them to a supper?"

Today at lunch Adam Geiger arrives with a bouquet of fancy Dutch tulips for Aunt Ilona: "For the first of May!"

Alex starts to sing the Internationale!

"C'est la lutte finale . . ."

Uncle Newman: "Not even as a joke! Please!"

Perl: "Well, dear heart, you would have

done us all a better service if you had brought the bulbs. *At least, we might be able to eat them.*"

In our hiding place beyond the garden, today I had almost convinced Alex and myself of the authenticity of his possession of me when there raced through my mind the image of the Communist woman again. She had said to me as I departed: "We know you are intelligent. Why do you cling so stubbornly to your own ignorance?"

Half-naked, I started up, with Alex still sprawled across me. My poor cousin probably thought he had blundered in some particular of his amatory technique. Wonder what he would say if I were to tell him of the Communist lady.

I waste time. Nothing is accomplished, not even writing in this diary. Alex distracts me somewhat. I am distracted chiefly by myself. Who am I? What am I to be? Where are we headed? I think and think about such matters until, as luck would have it, I prefer not to think at all.

It worries me—all this thinking. What am I planning? Up to? It's not that I distrust anybody, but I am, notwithstanding, making the firm resolve to observe, to note down everything, even the most trivial things. And, if possible, to be industrious in my interpretations of the various events. Only in that way will the time pass less slowly and painfully until such a day as we can know, can really know, what it is that is happening to us here.

Now what do we know? What do any of us know? It worries me. I am sure we only think we know certain things, but that is because we do not consciously take the pains to look about us. And so I shall be industrious and observe. It is the only way for me, even if it is all trivial nonsense.

A visit from the postal authorities. The International Red Cross has brought letters! A note from Cousin Fido in Geneva, discreet and well-wishing; a card from another cousin in Toulouse; a letter in American from Uncle Newman's brother which makes him wince when he stuffs the thing into his pocket. Of the first two he says nothing and peels off the stamps for his collection, but of the man Alex calls Uncle Bela, he comments: "My brother was always a scoundrel and he is no different even now."

Alex inquires: "Will we be allowed to reply?"

"Why, of course," Uncle sneers. "They are even planning to send us airplane tickets for the winter at Mentone." And with a loud laugh he leaves us.

The following things happened to me today:

I saw M.S. again and he is brazen as ever.

Uncle Newman informed me that there would be an auction sale of my parents' property.

Adam brought Perl a bottle of fermint and for Uncle a bottle of Ober-Salzbrun to drink with milk for the neuralgia over his eyes and nose.

I bested Alex in a competition for the diagramming of English sentences in which examples were drawn from the text of *Martin Chuzzlewit* . . .

And Aunt Ilona admonished me for stuffing one of the pipes in the water closet.

When I replied that it may have been another of the girls, one of her daughters, for example, she insisted that I was the only one who was recently having her "monthly."

I fritter my day away with small cares about everybody and everything.

Today M.S. came to the house with a letter for Uncle Newman from his father. Having glimpsed his arrival through the upstairs window, I remained in my room and would not come downstairs to speak with him.

Later in the day, Alex and I were together again. Most unsatisfactory, for Alex, if not for myself . . .

Today in Father Yagodah's study I read of the ordeal of Captain Alfred Dreyfus. How he stolidly maintained that the honor of France was bound up in his honor . . . and of those who worked resolutely for his exoneration—the exoneration of France—against a cruel, determined, and cynical opposition.

Such a cold person, the Captain. His wife —virtue maligned! They were not at all like our home-grown dissenters and radicals, but stolid bourgeoisie, as much concerned with the honor of France as their persecutors. Thus, it is obvious to me why Uncle Newman once found immense satisfaction in anti-semitism as history. Among his marginal notes to the author's chapter on the villain Esterhazy he has written: "The increasing popularity of several species of second-hand nihilism in our own day is probably responsible in a large degree for the decreasing function of the will among all the educated classes."

I am writing this diary in the language of our "enemies," English, to insure privacy . . . and oblivion. Presumably, it was for the same reasons that Uncle Newman chose to make his marginal notes in English. Perfidious Albion! To speak here in private in the language of Keats and Shakespeare is to insure that one's insularity *is* oblivion. Surely German or Russian would be more appropriate. Uncle Newman and Alex are true Magyars. They speak German, French, and Yiddish. They even speak Hungarian. Is there a concept for *will* in Yiddish?

Vorstellung, I believe, is the German word. But it is perhaps a good deal stronger than mere *will.* Or does it mean *concept?* Silly that I flee what is said to be my mother tongue to reside in a babbling ignorance. Surely Uncle Newman is familiar with both these concepts, but he chose *will,* as if to indicate futurity. One wonders when such a notation was made. The little Dreyfus book was published in France in 1921. Tiresome that he thought himself so contemporary when even in the good Captain's day the concept of *will* was, as they say, increasingly *recherché*.

The fact is at the very moment when Dreyfus was expiating French honor at Devil's Island the nihilist injunction had been given a new ferocity. Baudelaire was writing *"C'est affreux, o mon âme,"* and it was. Truly it was! And are we not now all pallid imitations of Monsieur Charles? This business about the will, I truly think it doesn't matter so very much; if it deflects one from thinking about courage, which is not a matter of will but instinct, it is even likely to be destructive. Nietzsche was correct: if one is ashamed of one's immorality it leads one to be ashamed of one's morality. Just exactly what have I to be ashamed about?

Never having kept a journal such as this, I am initially pretentious and this makes me write of myself as if ashamed. It's as if Uncle Newman had set out to compose love poems. I imagine he would try to spell out such things as *dynamo* and *modernize* in the acrostic. Thunderous grinding words! Yet there is so much to be said. To summon words is always dangerous, yet there is so much to be said. If I say I write because I seek silence, Friedrich Nietzsche would understand. Of all German writers his prose is the most lucid and sublime. It indicates the way to silence, that dim path beyond the thickets of will. Someday I shall read over what I have written, shocked that I no longer compose like a schoolgirl. *I am no longer a schoolgirl.* Rahel Varnhagen would understand; George Sand never . . .

It gives me pleasure to think that not even this record can survive the encroachments of our enemies. Using the present as archive, I am sharply aware that the present condemns me: *"C'est affreux, o mon âme!"* How such a statement pales to the point of seeming itself like second-hand nihilism when it confronts what is in store for us.

Prince Hamlet chose an antic disposition. It so happens it went poorly with him. My deceit is my apparent simplicity. If I were ever honest and open to a fault it would not go well with me. So I shall never let on what I know to be true. Never shall I declare myself. Never shall I forgive. Never completely give in.

As I was queuing up with Perl this morning beside the Jewish store, that Communist lady approached me once again. Distracted by gossip, Perl saw and heard nothing. The woman was staring at me frankly, like certain of those girls in school whom we knew to be Lesbians, although they also never once declared themselves. Like that girl who said to me that time: "You are one of us. We know it." I knew she said it, although we never spoke. Similarly, this woman was asking: "Do you wish to live? Do you even know if you wish to live?"

A few minutes later she was whispering again: "You *are* strong. You must be strong!"

It is a judgment with which I happen to agree, but from it I draw very different conclusions. I happen to be strong. Shall I be even stronger by surrendering myself to *them*?

The measure of my strength is that for more than a half year I have allowed dear Cousin Alex to do things with me knowing they would give me no pleasure. So there is your will, Uncle Newman. It exists to be violated so that it may be asserted once again by this human animal in dubiety and negation. I, who call myself a woman, have I no other strengths? It is because I am a woman that my negations still startle me, being so aggressive. Cousin Alex thinks we are to be married, and so we shall. Do the weak deceive knowingly, with malice aforethought? Cousin Alex is my safe conduct pass. For me, it is a joyous assertion of the will to surrender to him *so willingly*.

This diary is, therefore, a document about a girl, illiterate in a variety of tongues who seeks to preserve herself by wishing not to be a woman. I am that girl, that Lilo, and yet I also parody that Lilo, and I shall not even be that Lilo for very much longer. *"C'est affreux, o mon âme."*

Once, when we were together, Alex told me that he always envied women because they could have a man whenever they wished, whereas a man must always beg for consent . . .

I think that is generally true, truer than we women sometimes like to admit. It was because I wished to surrender that I did so with such seeming ease. Just imagine if Captain Dreyfus had ever succumbed to the self-pity of that distinguished pederast, Monsieur Charles. But, though Dreyfus and he were almost contemporaries, it was the stolid Alsatian Jew who risked the accusation that he was smug, cold, and unfeeling so as to assert his honor which is, of course, both the ultimate manifestation of feeling and the negation of that feeling. Poor silly Baudelaire, in love with his own mother. What did he ever risk beyond his Nancy soul?

Of course there is always the chance that I am mistaken. Cousin Alex claims I am always mistaken about these things. He calls me a blonde Cassandra. Let us suppose one could survive as outlaw. It is a genuine possibility. Do I have enough weakness to be strong in quite that way? Little Alex is a natural outlaw. He slinks around corners. He hides from himself. He is afraid of the depredations of his own shadow. Poor Alex . . . a lovable little outlaw who says to himself that he "loves" me. What is love? It is, I think, our contempt for the other which we then dare to summarize so by our feeling toward him as if . . . as if we were "in love."

Living next door to us are a family known as the Landers. My dueña Aunt Pepi, who has known the father well for a very long time, insists that they were once Jews. It so happens that they are not generally thought to be and have, therefore, escaped many of the restrictions which have been placed upon us.

My own opinion is that Aunt Pepi is generally correct about such matters of record. Her memory about matters of pedigree is almost infallible, a virtual Almanach De Gotha. Moreover, if the Landers do not know themselves to have once been, there would be no logical explanation for their behavior toward us. Not that they are cruel. They simply pretend we do not exist. If one of them sees one of us through a window or on the broad verge of their back lawn, he or she—all of them—quickly turn to look the other way. They even seem afraid of the complicity of a shared glance. Aunt Pepi says that the *alte* Lander, a very German gentleman, was once a playmate of my father. Perhaps he sees in me Father's face and that is what makes him blanch so and look the other way.

To see in me the face of Father is to return once again to the question of my beauty and/or ugliness. What am I really? Physically, I am fair, with fine features and exquisitely golden hair, but what else shows through? If all one sees is a beautiful face, it must eventually become ugly, a terrible unchanging mask. What is it that Alex sees when he stares at me so? I have often meant to ask, even during the act itself, yet have never done so. Why? For what possible reason? Would he be unnerved? Unstrung? Do I care? It is my terrible coldness again. Surely, my cousin and I owe each other more than just these hot stares and this recriminatory lust for each other . . .

Because I have been so skimpy the last few days in making entries in this journal, I decided tonight that I would write until I was groggy with sleep. Now I find myself still quite alert, but with little more to say. A asked me today if I ever kept such a diary, and I lied to him, no. If I had said yes, he would wish to read it. Not yet. Perhaps not ever . . .

To keep busy the entire family has set themselves various tasks: The Yagodah girls read *Memoirs of Comte Poniatowski*; Sarah's Maurice is absorbed by Shestok; Aunt Ilona has her whole library stuffed with magazines. I am browsing over a thousand different things . . .

The terrible rumors persist. Today Uncle Newman returned home from a Council meeting with a bruise above his left eye. He said some hooligan boy had mistakenly thrown a rock at him as he was crossing the market square. My uncle is afraid to call the Order Police. It seems we have no right to ask for their protection . . .

Later, while I was doing my chores in the kitchen, I overheard my uncle and aunt whispering. There is to be a general mobilization. It seems the authorities in Budapest are hard put to resist German influences. Some claim that the new government is merely a "front" for a German takeover and that our armies are shortly to be merged. Shall there be no sparing anybody? "But I am making plans," my uncle says.

"Plans . . . *what plans*?" My aunt's voice is always miserable and shrill of late.

Much later, she comes up to my room to

apologize for our argument of the other day about the stopped water closet. It appears that a large fat rat crawled down into the trap below the cistern and drowned . . .

A warm spring night. I have a dream. I am sleeping. A is next to me. I talk to myself in my sleep. The name of somebody. Another person. Once it happens when I touch Alex, the one who is next to me, but I awaken immediately, of course, with every kind of dread and loathing upon my lips.

Again I doze off, repeat the self-forbidden name, and awaken, feeling guilty. For me it is an agony.

I cannot let myself sleep and yet I am so drugged with fatigue. When I go to sleep there is that terrible name again on my lips that Alex will surely overhear, and if I lie awake I think to myself that I will be very sick.

Agony. Agony. I don't even know if I am

dreaming that I have said this name but I cannot allow myself to take the chance.

Alex and I spent virtually the whole sunny day behind the barn and I was very aware how desperately he was trying to please me. Indeed, he almost succeeded. I forgot the passing of time, the cast of his eyes, the unbearably heavy bearing down of his flesh on mine, the dark cold going of the spring sun, and surrendered to the pins and needles of a numb, quite contented endurance. If only I might continue to deceive myself so with him. Is it possible? With A I am continually aware of transience and pretense. We are like actors, absorbed within our parts. Our parts . . .

Because I am determined not to hurt my cousin, if I can possibly avoid it, I have decided to list below what I like and what I find objectionable about the fellow, as if I could, through this rational process, determine what reforms might be necessary to promote our future marital happiness.

(I have divided my *petit catalog* into five parts corresponding to looks, personality, attitudes and opinions, behavior, and what I must call, for a lack of any better word, ambition— i.e., his thoughts about what our future should be together.)

Herewith:

Looks: The physical appearance of my cousin-fiancé is altogether unsatisfactory, although not without a certain sweetness of expression and configuration.

A is small and slight. Physically, he barely towers over me. Surely he will be bald at an early age, for his hairline already recedes at not quite twenty-one and his complexion is sallow. Even after a day in the sun he does not redden, like his father whose skin is fair, but becomes a kind of unwholesome olive; and his beard is feeble, a smudge of dirty shadow across his jaw.

My cousin's lips compress tightly upon each other. They are also lacking in color. Only when he is disarmed by a smile, or some other unexpected emotion, is his face at all animated.

That animation, however, can be sweet and thoroughly disarming in itself. Smiling, A resembles a gentle scholar, absorbed by the sweet befuddlement of his studies. His long aquiline nose and big ears are rodent-like, but there is nothing mean or ferret-faced in the general configuration. A has the face of a clever little animal—at once greedy and self-absorbed, timid and implicitly involved with his own thoughts. Like his sister Perl, the eyes are rather too small and shifty. Again, it is not so much a fault of personality, I think, but of physical type. My fiancé has the look of the ghetto in his face. If there is sweetness present, it is the sweetness of a caged animal which no longer struggles to be free.

One stares at A and realizes that he must spend a great deal of his time attempting to please his masters; and that is perhaps why he is always looking at me so poignantly and yet greedily. It must be an agony for him not to know whether he has ever pleased me.

The caged animal is, as I said, slightly built; he does not appear to be strong; but his greedy little body is wiry and quick with certain violent inner gestures. There is a hardness to his flesh when I hold him against me which, I suspect, is vastly different from the firm but mature heaviness of his father. What thoughts! Why should I ever allow myself to care how his father might feel in my arms? With A I feel nothing and yet I am continually aware of my feelings, of physical sensations, sometimes pleasant, sometimes merely irritating. He does not, as it were, carry me away but tinkers over me, as if I were a stopped machine.

Personality: These are A's best traits: loyalty, intelligence, a poetry of verbal expression, and a discreet concern for the feelings of others.

A's best traits are more than balanced by his faults: a lack of physical courage; an inability to assert himself except through devious means; a certain mental pornography to which every act of love-making must be reduced; a refusal to confront himself; and, as Uncle Newman never tires of putting it, a tendency to fritter away his artistic gifts in dilettantish endeavors, a lack of either commitment or seriousness, if you will, so that he paints pleasing pictures, as if to please, and never seems to paint any better or any worse this time than before, now, or later.

You will note that I have described this second category under the rubric *personality* rather than *character*. In school we were taught to make a distinction between the two and I think such distinctions are generally valid. Thus Uncle Newman, whom I detest in many ways, must be described as a man of great character, whereas his son merely nibbles at the edges of certain vague personal aberrations. The difference is one of maturity. The father is predictable and strong; the son sweet enough but— like colored sugar water against a raw nerve —he manages to inflict pain through his very sweetness; and he never seems to know himself from one minute to the next.

To put it succinctly, A is not quite formed. He is like a child. It is his weakness and his charm.

Attitudes and opinions: I would describe my fiancé as a liberal with strongly conservative inclinations.

Now, to my understanding, there are really

two types of liberal-progressive in the world: those who wish to give everybody an opportunity to improve themselves, if they are strong enough, and those who wish all to descend to a nadir of lowness, a banality, a commonness of purpose and inclination, out of some inner weakness which they disguise, misguidedly, as the sense of fairness.

Cousin Alex approximates the latter type more than he does the former. His liberalism is tempered, I think, by a weakness of character which is nearly total, and by his strong contempt for all human accomplishments. He is bitter about himself, astonishingly so for a young man, and he is just a trifle cynical, although he lacks the fully developed cynical attitudes of Uncle Newman, a true conservative-progressive of the former type.

A exists to demean himself. He admires and envies his father but does not wish to ape him. M.S., I think, also admires the elder Yagodah as his father's successful rival in business, but there is this difference: for all M's brutishness and coarseness, the vulgarity of his ambitions, he is his father's son to the extent that he is intent upon getting back what was once theirs, and improving himself in the world and in his own personal standing with himself (that is the sum total of his envy of the present occupants of this mansion). Whereas A is certainly the more conservative in that he accepts himself as he is and tries to drag everything and everybody down to his level, by judging them insipidly and coarsely, by being so lenient, so liberal—if you will—in his regard of everything and everybody.

It can be said that Alex does not want for anything and that it is a fault with him. He takes his father's climb in life for granted and he is contemptuous of one who, like Miklos, has been made to suffer the humiliations of that success; and yet he is always so charitable, so magnanimous toward M. He condescends to pity the *goy*. Partly I believe it is fear; partly the falsest piety of all—his liberalism.

Nowhere does one see this more explicitly than in A's attitudes toward what we do together. If he wishes me to take enjoyment in the act, it is only another form of his reductionism. Through my pleasure I am to be reduced to his level. *I am to be like him.* A extends me pleasure liberally, as if that were my due. Never will I accept such treatment of myself, although I am also liberal enough that I do not like to permit myself denying him his "pleasures."

Behavior: A is committed to doing nothing. He is altogether cowardly. That is, perhaps, part of his charm. I also fear the strong-willed.

A seeks pleasure in everything he does. He is deluded, of course. There is no pleasure to be found with me. Neither to a life without purpose. What he achieves in place of the pleasures which he seeks is a dulling of the awareness of his boredom, that terrible insensate feeling of mere empty and mechanical behavior.

It is the same with A as a reader, I think. He reads a great deal, even more than I. But he is rarely moved by any emotions in what he reads beyond those of vague pleasure. Pierre Louÿs and Pushkin, they are all the same to him—a way of passing the time.

If I were threatened I sometimes think A would not protect me, and yet I know that his love of me amounts to a virtual adoration. A admires and adores me like the French verses he is always memorizing; it suits his fancy, flatters him to think that he and such eloquence can inhabit the same body, the same mind, the same tongue, but he would not protect me because it also flatters him to believe that he has dispensed with force, that he is somehow superior to its use, or, perhaps, because he would simply not allow himself to think in terms of such behavior. Strange. I truly believe A would try to be my consolation, even if he could not be my protector.

A says that he wishes above all to be a good painter. He paints better than most young men. He has a great gift for color and the subtleties of shading, but there is not a single bold stroke in any of his drawings. He is really awash upon his own sensibilities, an incorrigible *reveriste* whose best works suffer from a lack of conviction. Even those Conte self-portraits which were purchased at the Municipal Exhibition by the Rajks owe their charms not to any understanding of the medium but to his abilities to refine a blur into its formal components.

Of A, my sainted father used to say: "He will someday be Newman's cross." I believe

Father was mistaken. A may stubbornly cling to his sensibilities, but he is certainly not about to cause anybody a bit of trouble.

Ambitions: I find I have nothing to add to what I know about A's goals in life. Apparently, they do not exist. A is content to be exactly as he is. If only I knew what I found in common with him. For I am ambitious, but I do not have an inkling where my ambitions might lead me. Surely not to the commonplace pleasures which are A's. Then why do I allow him to take such liberties? Why have I encouraged him to believe, and why do I sometimes deceive myself into believing, that we can one day truly love each other? . . .

If I were simply a hypocrite my behavior might be understandable. But I sometimes have to excuse myself by thinking I believe in what I am saying. I think sometimes that I am every bit as weak as A and that I do not even have the strength to know my own mind about these matters so that, when we are together, I almost believe . . . *I would truly like to believe . . . and I do sometimes believe . . .*

Plain to see that character analysis is not my forte. If I am not to be another Madame de Lafayette, what am I to be beyond this beautiful face which has been inflicted upon me? Or am I again exaggerating?

When I shall get a chance to write again about these matters is hard to say. The weather has been unseasonably warm and beautiful, with flowers bursting forth everywhere prematurely and the ground alive with aphids; I have promised to pose for Alex for a series of sketches in oils, which I always find very exhausting. A is just now very cheerful. His father admired an imaginary scenic of the woods around the old summer house at Lillafüred, and he is a new man. He no longer stares at me as he once did. Obviously my ability to cast spells is as nothing compared to his father's sudden bestowal of approval. But, if truth were told, I thought his little scenic just a trifle banal. Well, we shall see what we shall see.

I return to writing with a heart full of joy. Nothing really has changed except that the world looks different and so I may have changed. I am happy and my happiness is as difficult to explain as my earlier feelings of dissatisfaction and uneasiness.

Permit me to digress, then, to explain that I am so unused to this fullness and joy that I am wondering if it can really be so. There would seem to be no measurements for calculating it, no instruments with which to understand what has occurred and what is now happening. And to make matters worse, I think my feelings have hardly been shared by my fiancé.

Strange. Half a week in which Alex and I have been rarely apart from each other for longer than a few minutes at a time and yet he wonders why I am so changed toward him. Perhaps he even confuses my feelings for their opposites. And yet I have been so tender and soft. I cannot be mistaken; I have been entirely unselfish, and not as before, not out of the need for self-sacrifice, but out of the most intense feelings of pleasure, of giving and being given in turn.

It is perhaps a bit banal when set down so. If so, I must be explicit. Alex is painting me naked behind the barn (that is to say I pose barely clothed and he renders me nakedly) and I am greatly pleasured by the act of posing. Not simply pleasured; I have been transfigured. I do not know myself in the postures in which he places me and I respond willingly. I see myself as he renders me, nakedly, and I enjoy the lapse of self-knowledge, yes, even the feeling of being cast adrift, confused, without any bearings on what I was and what I am for him, now, today.

Nor have I once been troubled by the possibility of exposure. When I pose I am somebody else. It does not matter what happens to this other person. She has no fears. Look. How beautiful she is. Look. How the artist stares so lovingly at her. Does he want her now? Then he will take her, of course; he must! Have the proper precautions been observed? Why should it matter? She is so happy. So far outside herself. It certainly cannot matter that she grows with the act and seems to live through it, breathing its strength through her until . . .

"Lilo, I am concerned that we may have been in too much haste . . ."

"We have had our pleasure," I tell Alex solemnly and pretentiously, "and now I shall have your child."

How lovely to be so banal and pretentious and not to be aware of it every minute. If only my fiancé would attend to his role in the charade, but he insists upon worrying and consoling me and he very nearly spoils my release.

"Alex," I tell him, "I am sorry about nothing. You must believe me when I tell you that I am not one bit sorry, but, on the contrary, I am . . ."

It makes him blush to hear how I am, but, for the moment, I go on posing and he is painting. There is nobody and nothing in the vicinity of our passion but our imagined selves and the heat of the day and the distant whispers from the elders.

I have a birthday. Even a woman of my not-too-advanced years should not be forced to divulge what number this is.

I shall not worry about anything today. It's my birthday. In the looking glass I imagine I can detect crow's feet.

That this should be happening to us now must sometimes seem incredible to Uncle Newman. He has lived here all his life, his father before him, too, and his whole life, his highest dream, was a struggle to be where he is now. Not our dreams, no, but his dream—to have the respect of others, to be a man of substance. Such a fever went into the getting of all this from Skirzeny and the others. Such a satisfaction it must have given him. One can see it in the way he allows liberties to that pig Skirzeny even now. It is always Uncle who allows the liberties; Skirzeny never takes a single thing . . .

And it must soon change. No matter, it

must soon change. Of that we are all sure, even Uncle Newman. He is like a man walking across a wooden bridge that has crumbled plank by plank into a raging torrent as he crossed it, so that he can go neither forward nor back. Ahead lies a savage uncertainty; behind he has turned all into oblivion.

Strange, Uncle of all of us is the only one who seems to worry about the future. One can see it in the way he looks at his son Alex as if to wonder: Can I trust him with all this?

That this should be happening to him now, it's truly incredible. As a child, I always thought Uncle the strongest in the entire family. Even though we were socially more advanced, I always knew he would someday have the edge on us. And now *this . . . incredible*!

Even to me it is hard to believe. I am not a person who expects unreasonable things out of life every day in the week and when they happen, as now, as they have been happening for so long, it makes the prison in which I was content to live intolerable. I wish to break away, to escape. I fever after freedom. How? Where? When one doesn't know what is to be . . .

I fever after freedom in part because I am so intolerably lazy and listless, I think. We girls are taught early that we are to be this way. *They* demand it of us. There is always this disappointing destiny awaiting us, a kind of tawdry humiliation which is not to be avoided. It *is* not to be avoided. And so we grow bitterer and bitterer even as we pretend to fever after our imaginary freedoms.

If only I could someday see myself as wife and mother, perhaps I would no longer fever so. But when I see myself this way I am ashamed. It is the thing I can never tell Alex. It is a shame and a humiliation for me to be so yielding to my destiny, and I fear it would murder something in me if I made myself unyielding.

We have a visitor: Victor Unsgrabber who is a grand-nephew of the first wife of our common grandfather, Istvan Fass. A strong young man with workmen's hands and shoulders;

Victor's family were living in a village not far from Mishkolz. He is not quite eighteen, a handsome peasant boy with a look of exasperated anger on his face. Uncle Newman welcomes him warmly, and we are soon called to the table to take tea. Victor tells us he has come to us with forged papers by way of Bratislava. He also tells a queer story of what happened in his village shortly before he departed.

A gang of Jewish boys of which he was a member petitioned their elders: if any further deportations took place, they were prepared to burn down the old ghetto with benzine as a mark for all of Europe that Jews were not going to be pushed around any longer. The Jewish Council hears of this and orders them to its offices: "If you set fire to any one part of the town, the whole may go up in flames, and we cannot allow this to happen to our innocent countrymen."

Victor is very bitter about the burning affair. He tells us he cannot be sure that his parents are now alive. He tells us that he plans to join the partisans in Croatia. He asks that Uncle Newman inquire after his family through the proper representations but he will not accept Uncle Newman's offer of money. Toward Alex and myself he is particularly bitter: "Surely you must see the future clearly," he tells us, before departing, without even bidding goodbye to Uncle.

Victor is even unintentionally cold to his aunt. When she hands him a parcel of food and clothing, he says: "Your stepsister should be very grateful."

Aunt and Uncle now take rhubarb tablets after every meal and my aunt is always administering oil enemas for herself and poor Newman. Even I am chronically constipated. Perhaps it is the new rations, a matter of diet, they say.

Cousin Victor's visit has left a pall over all of us. Immediately afterward, Uncle Newman departed without telling any of us where he was going. Then I went out to pose for Alex. Twenty minutes later, the elder Skirzeny arrives. A little black-marketeering matter, I suppose. We see him with Uncle Newman, framed within the leaded windows of the study. Alex and I have nothing to say to each other. We are finding it difficult to concentrate on work. Presently, I excuse myself to go upstairs. I am not feeling well (the sense that my "courses" are coming on again). The dull slow ache of imaginary menstrual pains . . . I do not come down to supper . . .

I pass one of M's younger sisters on the street. She is off to do housework in the gendarmerie. Magda told me. Poor thing . . . Her father had servants once, like we once had them, and now the former occupant of our house sends his daughter off, thin and consumptive-looking, to do housework among the bumpkins who will be sure to take advantage of her, too, if they possibly can.

Is it any wonder that they hate us all so

much? But why? What have we done to impoverish them? We Jews do not make the social conditions. We, like them, are the victims of such conditions.

Does anybody know our Sarah? Does Sarah even know herself? A's sister is so sweet, so selfless, so different from all the rest of us. Is it a mask or is it real? Could anybody be like her and not feel humiliated to have to live among us? What difference does it make? *She is.* She lives with us, a constant reminder of decency. We must all love her for that, even her brother and sister.

A thought came to me today as I was strolling near the arbor.

The difference between Uncle Newman

and our so-called enemies is not so great as some would have us believe.

By conviction, intelligence, and passion, they are all dedicated opportunists.

Whereas the difference may lie chiefly in the fact that the latter have seized their opportunity at the expense of the former.

※

The visit of Victor Unsgrabber lingers on unpleasantly. Today in the garden Alex asks me: "If you had been asked to choose whether your father or your mother were to live, how would you have chosen?"

I do not reply. The question seems crude and impolite. Choose how? Why?

I say: "Such choices are impossible . . ."

"My father would know how," Alex replies. "You can be sure of that."

"Your father would always choose a dear one such as you or your mother."

Afterwards, I feel very tired with myself and just a little sick to my stomach. For the first time, I worry if it is possible that I am pregnant.

In the evening the whole family plays bridge. Aunt Ilona chatters a great deal about how she plans to bake her own bread.

I am not pregnant. ~~My "monthly" has arrived nearly a full week premature.~~ I am almost disappointed to be a full week premature. To have a child is to assure oneself of love, I tell myself, but Perl, who is very observant and shrewd and always unpleasant, tells me that she has also been in ill-sorts and quite irregular over the past year. *"It is just nerves,"* she points out. *"Nothing but nerves."*

Alex is also disappointed that I will not lie with him as usual for the moment.

Strange. Saw M again today. Saw him the last time too . . .

Uncle Newman tonight gave us the following analysis of what is happening and what we can expect.

The war cannot last more than another year. The Hungarians are making "secret" contacts almost daily through the Vatican with the Allies. All Hungarian Jewry will be under Vatican protection no matter to what extent Germany takes over the administration of our armed forces. The Bolsheviks will not be allowed to pass beyond a certain point in Moldavia or above the Danube before a peace is negotiated between the Red Army and Hungarian partisans. Our best hope is in Hungary and the Vatican.

Strange. We do not seem to disregard the old man, but we no longer listen to him with the rapt attention which he could once command. We don't even ask the obvious: what secrets are these if you could know of them? We each seem to listen and to be thinking our own thoughts. It is clear from the unenthusiastic way in which Maurice and Alex, for example, argue with the head of the family. At one time, their arguing might have had sharpness and point, but now it is merely a rotation of facts to suit some other equally insipid prognosis.

Much else is happening about which I also should report, including a possible spat between Uncle and the old man Geiger, father of Perl's intended, and his nephew, Advocat Fry, but I shall save myself until tomorrow morning early, as I am so tired of late, so incapable of framing my thoughts with any cogency, and it is very late and Alex is asking to see me, and I wish to be with him too. It is so much nicer than this thinking up of useless thoughts.

One time Uncle Newman wrote with his own solid idealism about "harnessing the peasantry to productive labor."

Now these same peasants scheme and connive to harness him to the guillotine.

Am I sorry for him?

No I am a contemptible little nasty . . .

and I am so upset with myself most of the time that I can only resort to irony, which is the ignorance of the modish mind.

In French they say *"les extrêmes se touch-ent."* How very apt that is in describing what has been going on between Cousin Alex and myself. That we are entirely different in every respect as people, it cannot be denied, as different as beauty and the beast. We are the radical extremes, as well, when it comes to our personalities, which I believe I have made clear, yet we are being drawn closer and closer together by events like the circumference of a circle which bulges far apart only to come together again at a point in space.

Not only do I no longer reject Alex, I seem to enjoy the humiliation which is concomitant to our frequent coming together. Yesterday we made love, even though I was not yet rid of my affliction. Afterwards, Alex wanted to interrogate me about my feelings. I started to tell him that he was being nosey, but could see that he would respond with a look of hurt, and so I answered his questions as fully as if he were the gynecologist in Budapest and later submitted once again, not without pleasure. It was only the fact that the Skirzenies were expected that made us withdraw from one another.

The extremes touch each other equally, I am afraid, with Uncle Newman and his son. I know of no two persons who are so opposite and yet conjoined. I sometimes even think my uncle is aware of what his son is doing with me and that he approves, out of a feeling that he will gain some further advantage or power over me that way. But, while I do not really believe what I am saying, I do believe that Uncle Newman and his son partake of certain particular covenants regarding our future here. They will certainly never betray each other. Of that I am certain.

Oh, if only I could explain what I meant, if only I knew. My uncle is not the sort of man to be trifled with. Does he despise me? No!

Only my weakness and my beauty. I must be strong then if only so as to be the more beautiful and weak.

What nonsense I talk. My beauty makes me ugly? I am weak and ugly and Alex has the strength of his father. He has this crutch and can depend upon it. So can the others. Only I am alone in this household, like some prisoner in Count Petofi's castle. I must get to know my own mind and decide how I must act. I cannot afford to take my pleasure in weakness any longer. Alex and his father are scheming against me. I am certain of it. I have succumbed and now they are scheming together. Who will help me? To whom can I turn?

I have decided to destroy this diary today or, at latest, tomorrow. I will be sharp with them, also, and I will not for one single moment let on that I am wise to their little tricks. Toward Alex I shall be as correct as any Budapest whore, although he shall not have me again. He shall never have me as before. I cannot trust him, for it is clear that, despite all, he is really just his father's son.

I know this from a thousand different

things that have passed between them. Yesterday we lay together quite harmlessly beneath the big shade tree on the back lawn. Overhead branches stretched like blackened veins in some vast articulated body of the sky. The leaves wore tiny clots of moist green through which the sun barely shone. Our thoughts were of ourselves, yet we spoke of each other and of our friends, our parents, our families. Alex told me he was thinking of painting a group portrait of his entire family and I said I would help him arrange them as they should be posed. He was more ambitious than I have ever known him. He said he wanted to paint the sky from beneath the tree just as we were seeing it now, lying as we were, and he said he would like to paint somebody, a figure perhaps of a God, perhaps of a bird, in flight above the branches . . .

How lovely it all might have been. Not being able to look into each other's eyes, we talked with perfect candor. Nothing escaped our conversation. We were then truly lovers, although, as I say, we did not even touch, and I was also aware throughout of our puniness, of how we lay like tiny illicit figures against the warm earth. Yes, I actually seemed to see us together as separate from our physical beings, a tiny tableau of figures beneath the awesome darkening sky. We may have been only fifty meters from the back windows of the house, but we seemed as remote as figures in a cinema picture, viewing ourselves as we talked, talking as we viewed each other.

And what if the muskiness of damask roses which covered everything, including us, was only momentary, a product of the changing wind, we were, nevertheless, true exotics to one another. Alex even spoke of M. S., and of his ancient feelings toward him of loathing and envy and I confessed, albeit obliquely, that I did not find Skirzeny's eldest altogether repulsive. "He is cruel and even crude," I said, "but he is not altogether stupid or unattractive."

For, you see, we were not talking to each other but to two rather perfect images of frankness and intimacy whom our reclining figures happened to resemble. Yes, we were the voices of these two miniatures who seemed to be floating beyond us on the musk of the spring day.

Permit me simply to point out that our conversation seemed timeless, although scarcely half an hour had passed since the factory whistle recalled the workmen from their lunch pause, when I became aware of a cold shadow across our bodies and, looking up, saw the great figure of Uncle Newman. He had his hands squarely knotted behind his back so that his portliness protruded. He spoke with his sly wink: "So you have not been working all this time. I begin to perceive that I must give you both chores."

"Not at all, Father," Alex rose up, "I was telling Lilo of my plans. There are many paintings I wish to do. Lilo is a great help to me in deciding which. You do understand, Father . . ."

And so on. And so forth. The silly fool could not bring himself to stop apologizing when it was clear, after all, that there was no need for him to do any such thing.

"It isn't as if Lilo were merely wasting away the time. We talk about very serious matters, and she is, as I say, a great help to me, Father, in making plans. She is very sensitive to what I'm about. Don't you see? Oh, but of course you do. You must. You do see, don't you, Father?"

I am exaggerating, too, of course. Alex is never quite that abject, although almost so. And what is the point of apologizing for wasted time now and to such a man—our betrayer? It can only mean that he is himself prepared to betray . . .

No. I refuse to believe any of this of Alex. I must destroy this diary. I cannot allow myself to think these things of the man whom I am engaged to marry.

On a clear morning all one's murky evening resolutions come to nought. It is the loveliest day we have had in some weeks, a sky of purest azure and the air like the warm breath of a child. I woke up lighthearted. I can actually see the peaks of the mountains, the pass winding up toward Szeged, the village of Gidelve.

Clouds below the mountains . . . alabaster
. . . lost in alabaster clouds . . . all this . . .

Indeed, I can even make out the tiny hair-like contours of fern trees and hemlocks that bunch together across the verdant slopes in densest sage greens. Beyond, lie the higher mountains, empurpled in haze, but these foot-hills define themselves for me now in the bright sun. A cart winds up a pass, dust sifting up from its wheels to fuse with the little tufts of spring cloudlets which even now lie below the brow of these hills like rich veins of alabaster or, per-haps, whitest toffee. It will not remain clear the whole day, for the cloudlets will rise above the hills and swell and blacken and then rain will fall. How I wish I could describe the long-ing I feel to be among those hills, hidden by such soft thick tuffets of cloud, to merge, as it were, with the profound silence of distance, to be away from here at last. . . .

A did a cartoon today for his ambitious family painting. I mean the group portrait: A pack of birds about to peck one another. When the modeling becomes tedious he wanders off angrily, comes back a half hour later wishing to make love, but I refuse by sending him back to work again on faces, shoulders, and hands.

A queer observation from the poet Valéry has set me thinking in savage terms. Suppose that a cure for cancer were devised and it was found that the patient must sate his malignancy by consuming living human flesh . . .

I don't know what to make of any of this so I shall try to put it to the back of my mind, as with all my resolutions. Last evening I swore never to write in this day book again. This morning, the usual troubles with A and I am so alive to the possibilities of my prose that I find it difficult to keep up with my scratching pen.

I was with A all evening long. He read to me from *La Jeune Parque* and then we walked in the misty garden to our "nesting place." We said very little to each other, merely attempting to cover ourselves from the evening dampness. Nevertheless, I came to see how I have misjudged my young beau. He is exceedingly solicitous of me and cannot do enough to please me, and once again he stares and stares, transfixed by my physical beauty. If only he knew of the mistrustful soul dwelling within.

It was nearly dawn when we separated again and in the soft, wet, heavy air I allowed him to kiss me lightly on the lips before taking his leave. I said it would be better if we were to enter the house separately, but I had really other plans in mind. I hoped to violate Uncle N's study, not to snoop, but to acquaint myself in the finest detail with my actual circumstances vis-à-vis bank accounts, investments, etc.

Fifteen minutes or more I waited in that cold misty dawn, feeling very much like an intruder when, at last, I had the temerity to sneak up the back stairs into the warmth of the scullery. By then, the mist was invading even the rooms downstairs. They all seemed cobwebbed with greyness and wetness. Nothing stirred within those webs, not even the flutter of a moth's wings, although I stopped many times, startled by the gnawing of what I took to be a mouse.

Within the great dining hall a hush lay over everything, too, as if the family were all still assembled, waiting in polite silence for some particular new course in a long mournful repast.

We had set the table for breakfast that very evening, as was customary in the Yagodah household, and there was a slight sweat upon all the utensils and dishes, which were also mottled, of course, by the heavy greyness of dawn seeping in through the musty air.

I stole my way to the door of Uncle Newman's study, but could go no farther. I honestly felt as if a great hand was on my shoulder, restraining me, reproaching me, urging me not to step across that threshold.

But my hand was on the knob, and it easily turned to admit me. I did not go forward. I simply could not bring myself beyond this intention to the act itself. I stood shrouded in greyness, chilled and uneasy, and did not move forward or back while the great clock in the square chimed the hour. It would soon be morning. Still I did not move. Whatever lay beyond the door, across that broad cluttered desk or within any of its drawers, I preferred not to know about. Then why had I come this far? Why didn't I go about any of my business? It would soon be morning and I might be detected . . .

Still I did not move. Again the clock tolled and the hour was later but I had no feeling of the passage of time. It was as if my heavy feet were lodged in the spot, a stiff figure out of one of A's paintings, as if my body was encased in the waning greyness of the musty air. I had long since given up the idea of escaping. I would stay. I could not enter and I could not leave. I seemed to be waiting to be observed. I seemed to wish to make of my presence upon that threshold a kind of warning to Uncle Newman and to the entire household.

It was Sarah's Maurice who found me there. He had risen early because of their little Anatole and was proceeding downstairs to mix pabulum. He saw me and perhaps his eyes boggled, as if confronted by some queer new piece of statuary, but, as always, he was very gentle with me: "You are up early. Is anything the matter?"

I told Sarah's husband that I had been awakened by what I thought was the sound of an intruder, and had gone to investigate. God help me. Despite myself, I was stammering even as I improvised . . .

"An intruder? How? Where?"

Above us on the first landing of the stairwell stood Uncle Newman: "Did you say you heard an intruder, child? At this hour? Why, it's almost morning. Surely it was your imagination. Or perhaps it was one of the family . . . a little restless . . . *one of us you thought you heard.* . . . Good day, Maurice. I see you have risen early, too. Playing at father, are you? Is Sarah not well?"

My uncle's face was rigid with irony, his lips firmly pressed against each other as if not to emit the chance of an amused smile. He came down the stair and took me gently by the hand away from the study door: "Never fear, child. I shall investigate this intruder of yours. In the meantime, I advise you to go to your room."

I did as I was told, and lay in bed reading *From the Good Land* without giving it any attention until such time as I heard the matutinal voices of the family at the breakfast table.

After breakfast, A met me in the scullery. "We shall have to be more careful," he said. "Father has told me of your 'intruder.' Next time I will make sure that you go up to your room first."

Although I was vexed with Alex, I found myself agreeing to his proposal that we meet after second breakfast in the attic to select frames for some of his new paintings. Uncle Newman keeps a file cabinet in the attic containing records of many of his financial transactions. Perhaps I can cajole A into snooping with me.

Question: Is it possible I refused A today because of my vexation of last evening?

But when I saw him this morning after second breakfast . . .

A strange and terrible thing has happened. I do not know what is to become of me. I do not know . . .

About M my lips remain sealed. I cannot bring myself to write of it. I shall never write of it.

What has happened has happened. Now only our vindictiveness lingers. Still I cannot bring myself to write of any of it, just as I also cannot bring myself to talk of it. It has happened. Let it be.

Uncle and Aunt's wedding anniversary. For the whole day she stays in her room and weeps alone. I feel as if I would like to go to her, but my heart is so heavy on my own account—how could I help?

There is a kind of hell in my heart. My head and heart have never stopped aching. Alex, Alex, such distant relations between us have never existed before, yet I cannot bring myself to forgive . . . to go to him.

I keep to my room all day.

In the evening I feel fresher and go for a stroll in the garden. A is away from the house with his father . . . an errand.

For my morbid, sad face Aunt Ilona prescribes an aperient, which I take but it does not act, and I go to sleep in my clothes. In the middle of the night I awake. I feel fresher, go down to the pantry, eat pickled mushrooms. It is a delicious feast, but my stomach is now quite upset.

What a terrible pain I have in the back of my head too. Such as the pains my mother used to have. Alex, Alex, am I to have a nervous stroke?

M has sent an insulting note. What is expected of me? What am I to do? A is outraged, although he has no right to be. Did he bother to defend us? Then he has forfeited the right to judge me in any way. As for M. S., his particular brand of truth-telling is so crude that, of course, he is not completely in error. Jew sow he calls me after everything is over, but does he dare to say what he thought of me when we were together?

No. It is all horrible and senseless. There was a momentary thrill of pleasure, yet I can honestly tell myself it wasn't me; it was some other person. Moreover, why must I defend myself? I was not the one who did anything to anybody.

I sometimes think Uncle Newman knows what has happened. The whole household seems to know that A and I are at grave odds over something. Could his father know even more? Could that drunken old goat, Farnas S., be telling tales to him about his son? Would he dare to boast? Would the son, perhaps, be bragging of what he did to me? Alex must sense many of these same things, for he continually approaches me in his timid way, as if he would like to speak of these matters. Alex dear, I cannot; perhaps I never shall. Half a week has passed and yet I feel as raw as if the encounter were still fresh.

I did not sleep all night and am within a hair's breadth of suicide.

I have been poring over Uncle Newman's legal dictionaries for definitions of the concept *to rape, to violate.* It is apparent that the lexicographers are deeply puzzled by such terms. Is the right of the woman to resist conditioned by the state of her chastity? Can a woman be raped more than once? If she has ever derived pleasure from the act, can enforced pleasurement fairly be called an act of rape?

No! It is simply not possible to talk of these things in the abstract. Not ever possible, I say.

A noted German lexicographer has even pointed out: "Virtue is violated whereas a woman who has known men merely succumbs . . .

"To feel desire," the learned fellow further points out, "is to deny the rigorous commandments of the masculine will."

Indeed, he even argues: "It cannot be seriously maintained that every act of lust perpetrated against womankind is rape, else prostitutes would be the reservoirs of abused virtue and the lowest streetwalker in her squalid alleyway could maintain, *post coitus*, that she had been abused."

It is clear from all I have read and all that has happened to me, of late, that to be a woman is to succumb to the most callous definitions of stupid and unfeeling men. It is our fate, like our beauty, a terrible destiny.

Alex, Alex, a man forces himself on you and you feel desire and then you are to assume that you have led the fellow on? It is all so callous and cruel. Men make laws to suit their needs and fancies and then punish us through them. They are allowed to be the arbiters of their own force, *whereas we* . . .

What wickedness . . . We are condemned to be weak and to be condemned when we reveal our weaknesses . . .

Even my cousin, who is hardly a man, condemns me so. At the moment, he seems most concerned about the possibility of disclosure, although he has also made it clear that he would be distraught if I should become pregnant.

Yes, A is hardly even a man, but he lives in the world by the rules which men make, and he shares in those bigotries which are the condition of all men. Alex, I will admit I was not as repelled as I should have been, for the thing was happening beyond the quivering figures who we then were. Thus, if I was made to feel desire, is it because I am unpure? Must I also humble myself to apologize like a whore?

I cannot bear to look at A when he stares at me that way, as if he saw only my dirtiness. What does he expect of me now? To another I might say I was overcome and you did not protect me, but he would not be convinced. He saw us. He observed us. He thinks he has the right to judge. And when I judge him in my sterile anger, he pretends that he is outraged. Alex, even you cannot be allowed to deny that there was force used. You must not be allowed to deny such a thing.

How I wish that I knew more about the physiology of the act itself. At school we were taught only about childbirth and the husband's rights. Pleasure was never denied but it was never stressed. To have questioned Aunt Pepi would have been like questioning that German lexicographer; if she is not still a virgin, it can only be an accident.

What is happening to me when I feel desire? Can it be that with M I was merely exorcising the lust which Alex, half-man that he is, was the first to arouse in me? Why then, of course, I am not to blame, not even from a technical point of view. A took his satisfaction at my expense and, like some aroused mare, I was made ready for this other . . .

I shall have to read more about all these things. *How? Where?* The other girls can be of no help, of that I am sure, and Aunt Ilona would blush to speak of such matters. If only I could question streetwalkers or peasant girls. They would surely know and they would speak so that I might understand.

Alex, I am coming to think that we have made up rules so as not to offend our sense of human dignity, as if that dignity could be said to exist even beyond the existence of these rules, when it is clear to me, even though I am a woman, that men (and I include my sex in the corporate noun) are capable of every infraction as normal beings; and that it is only the abnormal who hesitate at all. Witness this evil time, these evil and mendacious people, this house, this lust, and the blindness of our fate.

A has lost a very valuable cigarette lighter in the woods somewhere. He thinks it happened *that day*. Would I go with him to look for it? No, I say, but immediately go off beyond the back gate by myself and pick lungwort, golden cowslips, and some other mysterious yellow flowers which, in English, I think, are called bread-and-butter.

In the back field I notice many small dead birds and animals. I have heard that *they* are using noxious gases on the wildlife to test them for the front and that whole forests have been depopulated, but one hears so many things. It may simply be a part of the diurnal processes.

Afterwards I come home, the same as ever. Seeing me, Aunt Ilona wonders if I am consumptive. She wishes to send a sample of my phlegm to the apothecary Geiger. "Your color is simply awful," she insists.

I tell her Alex and I have had a spat. "It happens," she says, "and you must not grieve over it."

I should like to remind her of the crying I heard behind her door on her wedding anniversary, but I say nothing.

I am taking a special tea made of herbs for my color. It does little good, but leaves a bad taste in my mouth. My condition in general: lifelessness, idleness, depression.

I think too much and my thoughts are quite loathsome to me. And if I try not to think, I am no better off. If anybody ever would say to me that I should still know lust, for example, should still imagine these things, what terrible words I would spit out at such a person. I am humiliated by my self-knowledge. The real Alex repels me even to talk, but I still imagine, still remember, the A I once knew and the things we did together, and I sometimes remember M even though he did these things to me in the presence of A . . .

Haunted by such memories, I continue to loathe myself and wander about the house, as if

to escape my own shadow. I do not wish to
see or to speak to anybody, yet I cannot be
alone with myself. Then I must surrender once
again to these loathsome imaginings which I
can no longer stand in myself.

The last few days I have been a great deal
with Uncle Newman. He seems unusually pale
and worried. It is clear that his affairs do not
go well. All the more surprised am I that he is
suddenly so friendly, so gentle, with me. Sometimes in my wanderings I come to the door of
his office and enter the room. Uncle Newman
must know it is me, but he does not stop what
he is doing. With a nod of that fine grey head
he instructs me to be seated. I fold my hands on
my lap and surrender to the scratchings of his
pen. Occasionally he glances up to observe me
and nods to himself as if to say, "Just so . . .
just as I might have expected," but there is a
softness to his glance that I find reassuring, as
if he knew all and did not judge me badly.

Yesterday he said: "I like to look up and see you here. You may come any time you like."

"It is so peaceful," I said.

"For you perhaps." He smiled.

And this morning after breakfast he reminded me with a quiet but firm voice: "May I expect a visitor today?"

But, when I entered the room and sat down, he did not so much as utter a word of greeting, merely glancing up to note that I was there with that soft gentle smile which is so becoming yet such a rarity with Uncle Newman.

I asked: "Can I help you, Uncle?"

"You are helping me, child," he replied, "more than you know." And he went on with what he was doing.

It is clear that I have cruelly misjudged the old man. He does what his interests urge him to do, but he is not dishonest, not a thief, and he is strong, and we need his strength now when we are all so weak. I gather my uncle is helping to frame a petition to the authorities offering the resources of the total Jewish Community to offset the terrible costs of the conflict. More than once he has glanced up toward his bookshelves to recollect some passage of law or a point of legal usage. Once Maurice came to the door to announce that a parcel had arrived and my uncle asked: "Tell me then, are you prepared to serve your mother country in arms, if necessary?"

"To fight for Germany?" The long-suppressed radical spirit in my future in-law flushed to the surface of his skin: "You must not be serious."

Uncle Newman replies: "Germany is one thing, Hungary another. You can serve Hungary and not Germany. Or do you think these Bolsheviks will run up to you and kiss you when they see you?"

A says nothing about any of this. I wonder if he is even being told anything. I know he too wanders about the house aimlessly, but he will not enter his father's rooms when he is there. Is he still so afraid of the old man? Or has he told him things about us which he is now ashamed of?

If so, Uncle Newman doesn't seem to be judging. He acts. *He does.* We are all dependent upon his will. I overhear long-winded conversations on the telephone about trifles and am certain that he would never trust the prying ears of those at the Central Telefonique with anything of importance. What is he thinking and what is he doing? I dare not ask. I find myself trusting him. His constant bustle and activity assures me. The package which Maurice had announced contains gardening tools, a shovel, a pick, heavy cord, and iron boxes of nails. Has he some plan? He has drafting tools and makes queer little maps. Again I dare not ask what any of this means but sit with him silently, and occasionally he smiles up at me before departing on some errand.

"What has happened to my son these days?" he asked, this morning, when he took his leave of me, but his smile was suddenly bitter, knowing. He seemed to have no doubts about what had occurred.

I said: "Alex is going through a stage. We are going through some stage together which . . . which," I was stammering, "keeps us to ourselves . . ."

"I am aware of difficulties," Uncle Newman merely announced.

When he was no longer in the house, I got up and went into the garden. Alex was there, saw me, fled, his face queer with staring at me.

He left behind an oil sketch of which the less said the better. After staring at it a while, I turned away but stayed within the arbor, beneath a cloud of midges, dozing fitfully to awake whenever I felt the tiniest sting.

At last it started to drizzle and I went inside the house once again. The women were all upstairs. From the garden I could see the lights glowing in their windows, but, in Uncle Newman's study, the door was closed, although I had left it ajar. I pushed it open from the threshold.

Alex was at his father's desk, going through papers rapidly with his little fervent hands. The sound of the opening door startled him, but only momentarily. Before I could assert that I had caught him off his guard, he exclaimed *"This must be it"* and took up a book between his hands. I closed the door behind me softly.

"It is good that you came," he said then.

"Good that we can be alone here now. Father will not be coming back until evening."

Alex spoke with an unintentional shrill falsetto. He glanced up from the book, as if expecting me to comment on the picture he was painting of himself, and then, softly, smiled to release me from the obligation, but the light was so bad that I saw only shadows, splotches of darkness like print specks against his face. It made him appear so unhealthy, almost like another person. I said: "Have we anything to say to each other?"

"Be seated," Alex insisted, and his glance pointed to the very same tapestried chair where I had been seated all this morning.

"Lilo," he said, when I reluctantly did as he asked, "we cannot go on this way . . ."

I replied: "Do you think we shall be allowed . . . ?"

"You are so bitter with me."

"I do not mean to be. I am sorry. I am bitter with myself."

"You have no reason to be, Lilo."

"Alex, Alex . . ."

Even he must have realized that he was

saying very foolish things, for we lapsed into a silence during which I could hear myself breathing.

I sighed. A got up to come to me, but my glance deterred him so that he sat down again.

Finally, he spoke.

"It isn't as if I wanted these things to happen. . . . Don't you think I am as unhappy as you? We must adjust to this new thing. If we love each other, as we say, we must try to be the better for it."

"The better for rape, Alex?"

"Not that," he reddened, "but afterwards. One must always go on. I mean it is just not possible that we should give up on one another without trying . . ."

"Trying what?" I asked.

"Lilo," he was growing darker, "it is not possible . . . it is just not possible . . ."

I really can't remember all that he continued to say, and I was so disturbed that I can't, with any certainty, remember how he said some of these things. Why did he feel such a need to justify himself to me? Did he think me stupid? Alex, don't you know I happen to share many of the same sentiments, but I also happen to know why they are all trivial and useless?

As A spoke today of our love and our duties toward each other, I was thinking of lust. The image of Miklos and myself flashed through my mind and I saw Alex standing helpless to one side. Our duties to each other, indeed! I felt very sorry for my cousin, for his words came from him in a shrill voice, awkwardly and painfully, making his face even more dense with shadowy lines of worry, but I could not bring myself any longer to listen to these words. Even as he spoke I got up and started for the door. I think he was still droning on as I began to mount the stairs to my room, but of that I cannot be sure.

Today another note from Miklos. It is a good thing it went unobserved. I can fool myself no longer about that boy. He is a brute. He insults me. He seems to wish to spit on me. It is his chief pleasure, no doubt.

Afterwards I went to Uncle Newman's study so as to seek a calm refuge. My uncle did not even glance up from his writing. If he knew I was there he gave no sign. I tried to think of what M felt he was doing to me, but my mind boggled. Is it possible I cannot understand this young savage? What are his demands on me? Why? Why do I not confess all to A? Am I in some way encouraging all this?

If I am, I do not know of it. He took me brutally and there was pleasure in the act, but it was not in the brutality; that all happened to someone else. In his letters he addresses me as "slut" and "cunt" and words I do not even understand; and he speaks of my "moist hot sow hole."

Strange to say, I do not even blush. It is as if he is talking of somebody else whom I envy more than anything else. It is only when my reveries are interrupted, as they were today, that I am at all upset by the experience, as if somebody has been eavesdropping on my thoughts.

Today a gentleman came to call on Uncle Newman. I did not recognize him, although it is plain from their conversation that he is no outsider to the community. They talk together in whispers at the other end of the room, and do not even notice me. On the way out the man stops by my chair. I am startled, embarrassed, and get up to leave. "Such a lovely young lady," he says. "Your daughter, Yagodah?"

"My niece . . . and future daughter-in-law, it is presumed."

"I wish you both well," the man says and he leaves.

Again we are alone together. My uncle's eyes glow fiercely. He says: "Did you overhear something? It is of no consequence, my dear."

He goes back to his scribbling. A moment later, he is glancing up at me again: "Perhaps you would like to sit by my side. You mustn't think that I shall protect you from Alex. Whatever happened is between the two of you. But I could be your friend, your confidant, if only you would let me."

I do not move any closer, saying: "I like it here, just as I am."

"All things change. They must change sooner or later," Uncle Newman adds. On his lips, the mysterious dim smile of the sensualist.

Nothing changing. Everything the same. Terrible!
Worse! Worse still.

A line from Marx, a favorite of A's:
"The invitation to abandon illusions concerning a situation is an invitation to abandon a situation which has need of illusions."
Ja, das hat er!

I sometimes wonder what would happen if I were to run away from here by myself. Where would I go? What would I do? I even dream about such things sometimes.

Last night I was running through a dark wood. A pursued me. He wished to make me "come to my senses." The gravel cut into our feet. My wrist ached and pulsed where he had tried to stay me by squeezing it, but I had broken away and was running all the faster, although he kept closing on me. At last I saw an opening between some branches in the forest that was only big enough for my body to go through. I pushed the leaves apart with my hands so they would not cut my face and raced on into a tiny clearing where M stood: "I am glad to see that you have gotten rid of your cousin."

He is as brazen with me as ever.

There is nothing good that I can report of my behavior of late. A and I go on and on, like figures in some fierce tableau, whether together or apart. The days grow longer, and I am constantly aware of the passage of time. I say little to anybody; all, except Uncle, keep me from their thoughts. Even him, I am not so bold about being alone with any longer. Not that I believe he will be a lecher; his senile eroticism is harmless enough; it's that I feel his competitiveness; his strength is truly oppressive; always he must be his son's father. He will always uphold Alex against me. It can't be any other way.

Beyond a doubt, what I fear most is M, and the people who are with him and encourage him, yet I believe, too, that I could talk to his kind now and that they would listen to me.

It's all silly nonsense, of course. I fear M because of the way he treats me, not because of what may exist between us. There are forces at work in him, I am sure, that are not so evil as others think. His grudge against all of us, it's real enough, God knows. Fancy that there *are* blood ties . . . wouldn't any man feel resentful of such perverted snobbery . . . the ways we have treated him and his family . . .

Aunt Ilona continues to concentrate on the state of our bowels: bilberries in cream, apricots, prunes, and last year's figs are about all there is to eat save for that fatty meat which I cannot bear to swallow. All the bread tastes like suet. Meanwhile, Uncle Newman keeps to himself and mutters continually to himself about the aperients or the bill of fare.

A German (Austrian?) officer has come to our house to inquire about billets. He is extremely curt but polite with all, introduces himself to neighbor Frankenauer, who happened to be present, as a family man, a grandfather, and consents to take tea while his staff car idles in front of the house.

The man's name is Stettinauer, born in Galicia near Czernow, said he knew my father's step-brothers there. Most polite he is, to a fault, but we could learn nothing from him about what is to be. He talks of arrangements, resettlements, population redistributions, but never goes beyond a single one of these vagaries to say how the cards may fall. When Uncle Newman presses him about this or that, the gypsy question, for example, he insists that he is just a billeting officer.

(Nothing personal against "the Israelites" as a race, he tells us, for hasn't he grown up among Jews?)

(The captain even expressed to us a certain war-weariness. He is, he says, lonely and homesick for his grandchildren, whom he should be dandling on his knee before the fire instead of this foolery.)

Another officer presently comes to fetch him. Of course, he has to put on then that he is being very correct with us.

Of late, I think a good deal about our fellow Hungarians. Are they like our friend, this captain? Do they know any better what is going on? Do they take sides? If you are fortunate enough to pass them in the street, they seem to stare at you as if you don't even exist, but, since the curfew, we see little of any of our neighbors. During the hour or so that we are allowed out to attend to business, only Jews seem to venture forth. The streets are deserted. We scurry about among ourselves like mice.

Tonight at supper Uncle Newman told us of his experiences with the Bosnian Uhlans during the Great War at Lespedíí. He has mentioned it all many times before, but never in such detail—how he was accepted as a comrade, of his wounds and of his commendation and of what his comrades-in-arms said to him then.

"Such ties cannot easily be severed," Uncle insists. He has forbidden any of us to fraternize with the Ukrainian constabulary forces. "Such people," he insists, "are savages now and have always been so . . . *un droit commun* . . . they are little better than convicts.

"But Hungary," he adds, "has had a great past and its future is assured. We must have faith in our countrymen. It is always the suspicion of disloyalty," he observes, "that is at the root of these crude anti-semitic feelings."

We heard gun fire tonight as supper was coming to an end, like a distant thunder, nothing more. A camp for training peasant militias is being established in the neighborhood of Dej. Or perhaps there has been a raid again on the new oil fields. We are certain it is no immediate threat to us.

After dinner, Uncle Newman must attend a Council meeting. Sarah and Maurice retire early. I am left to myself, for Alex claims he must attend to matters about the house, and I find a cozy niche in an empty guest room to write about the day's events. At first my pen refuses to flow of its own accord, so I have these groggy daydreams. Here is one.

I am invited to a great ball such as all the local nobility used to hold often before the war. My escort is an elderly Army captain. Alex will also be present, it seems, but he must escort his mother, since his father is away on business. We arrive at the great house in a staff car, hardly talking to each other along the way except to comment on the deep blueness of the sky and the numerous stars that have formed their constellations overhead. I recognize the bear, the hunter, the chariot, and am feeling rather proud of myself, and I look very lovely too, in pink *peau de soir* with white ribbons, a bouquet of marguerites and bluets which Magda's daughter has picked for me shortly before sunset. Gaudy perhaps . . . but lovely.

At the ball nothing extraordinary happens. I dance with all the young officers and drink punch with Alex, who is not, it so happens, a very good dancer. Only when we are about to depart and I have thrown my bouquet to one handsome young member of the local gentry does the gaiety suddenly fade and I have the sense of acrimonious talk from all sides.

"When does the Jewess perform?"

"I shall be disappointed if she does not live up to expectations. . . ."

"It is for her pleasure as well as our own. . . ."

My escort reaches out toward one of my ribbons and pulls on it. Presently I am coming unraveled. My gown has fallen to my ankles. I stand naked before the entire assemblage which is, of course, all very gay and silly once again.

"Do be natural," somebody is saying. "You must not blush in front of us."

Like a dummy, I do as I am told, and then am aware that the men are queuing up as if to take turns with me. They fuss with their trousers. One man approaches with a doll-like grin across his face.

"Use this," my escort declares. He hands me a cavalry sword. The man lowers his trousers, and I thrust the thing forward, vigorously, savagely.

Alex cries out: "Lilo, can't you see what you have done?"

The fellow is bleeding from the groin like a woman.

In still another daydream we are at Lillafüred, Alex, myself, and this girl from boarding school, the Lesbian (a very Jewish-looking girl) who was always making advances to me, but now she is attempting to flirt with A and I am very jealous . . .

I think I entertain these loathsome imaginings out of a sense of obligation. Obviously I have no shame, but would like to convince myself that I do.

A song heard through the windows facing onto the square:

> The great day is marching
> *marching*
> *marching*
> The great time advancing
> *advancing*
> *advancing*

Who cares if the roses bloom
Upon our graves tomorrow?
Roses plucked with joy smell sweetest
When they spring from rich soil.
The great day is *marching*
                    marching
Take courage. Be a good soldier.
Forward. Advance.

One of my Uncle's little *aperçus*: "Europe has survived every depredation except, perhaps, for those represented by its present generation of women."

Still another, from *My Impressions*: "God is the great provider for the poor. Those of us who are more fortunate should look occasionally to ourselves."

A third, a variation on the above which he has spouted of late at the slightest provocation: "It is a great tragedy that men no longer wish to be wealthy and women beautiful. Even worse than the Reds, I fear this mediocratizing of the image of Man."

An item from Aunt Ilona's inventory twists and slaps itself about in my mind like a snake of nonsense:

> 27 Rheingelder spoons *mit dem alten Kastanienbaum*
> 27 spoons with a chestnut tree

Why do I keep remembering chestnut trees which have never grown well here?

I wish I might see such spoons. But Aunt Ilona has put them away "in a safe place" until we are married.

> 14 Venetian bud vases
> 27 Rheingelder *Löffel*

Everything tucked away in their own safe places . . .

Lord God what are we doing to each other?

Lord God I don't wish to make myself into such a store room. Help me to forget

> *advancing*
> *advancing*

Somebody has been at this diary. I can tell. It makes my face burn to think of it.

I know because he (or she) has left cigarette ash among the pages whereas I do not smoke at all, as everybody knows. This person does: a heavy Turkish-style tobacco, to judge from the ash. It could have been Alex or his father or even Aunt Pepi. The stuff was pressed against the binding, a whole patch of it, like grey mold, and how it made me blush to see it, as if I had glanced up from a troubled sleep to find somebody staring at me. Who can it be? How will he or she reveal himself to me?

I cannot have imagined any of this. I know because the snoop has also left a dirty smudge of thumb print on my last entry. Am I not worth a moment's privacy? Whoever it was, thinks she knows certain things about me. Well, let her think. Let them all think. I know and I am not ashamed . . .

It has happened to me this way. The last twenty-four hours have seen Alex and me drawn more closely together again. Only last evening, his father, being out once again at another interminable meeting, I suddenly thought how cruel all my judgments have been of this poor lonely fellow, my fiancé. Nothing that has happened to me should be laid on his doorstep, I thought. For it is one thing to prevent, quite another to initiate, violence.

Knowing all this, I could no longer be so distant. I waited up for Alex in the corridor near the stairwell when I thought he should be retiring, and spoke to him: "Please, don't be afraid. Have pity on me. If I have said certain things, I am sorry. You must come with me now for I am truly sorry."

The silly fool honestly thought that I was trying to lure him to my room. He protested that he must wait up to admit his father. We quarreled. Even though I didn't wish to, I found myself saying things about his father and himself, about their motives toward me. Once, Alex came toward me. I slapped at him and fled up toward my room.

Immediately, I felt deeply ashamed again over what had happened. A feverishness overcame me. I was moved to pity for A and myself. I could not sleep. I played records on the Zimmerman of Cherubino sung by Shtoltz, but soon grew bored with all that. The night grew darker. I stayed at my window, staring out into the garden, even hoping that I might catch a chill in my feverish state and that it would all end that way; for I was so truly revolted with myself, you see. I thought that if Uncle Newman were to return home I might try to see Alex again. Yes, I would try to make it up to him. In the meantime, I must wait.

Be patient, soul.

But how could I?

I wished to run out as I was and fall into the rain puddle pond that has collected beyond the back gate of the house and there drown perhaps.

How was I to be patient feeling like this?

It was a night of strange alarms in which a distant reverberation of gunfire shuddered brilliant flashes of lightning off and on. Once I dozed off, waking with a quickening start at the sound of the front door closing. I went out my door toward the dark portion of the corridor from which I could look down and see all without being seen. A was coming through the front hall chatting with Maurice and then he looked up and smiled upon seeing me; and I was then smiling too, because I was so terribly happy to see him. And my happiness surprised me. I recall ducking backward farther into the shadows as Maurice came up past me on the stairs, and then again I glanced down and A was looking at me, and his look was questioning. When our eyes met I felt we were together.

Now, as I think of it, I realize that I don't really remember all that happened. I don't know why I felt like such a hurt little girl when A pushed me away from him, insisting that he had to wait up for his father, and why it hurts me so to think even now that he refuses to acknowledge my presence in front of his own brother-in-law.

For a moment I even felt jealous. But of whom? *What?* At last the house quieted and we stood as we had been, with this bright new happiness across our faces, until he came up the stairs once again toward me to offer his jacket for my shoulders so that I would not be chilled.

He said: "I will come to you as soon as Father is asleep . . . no matter what the time may be," and it seemed as perfectly right for him to be saying this then, as it did for me to be standing as I was, shivering and hardly clothed at all, in plain view of all the family's rooms at nearly one in the morning.

I started off then to retire once again, feeling such a sweet pleasure, I still don't understand why, not even now, when I recall it all; and, as I came around the great corridor, there was Perl:

"You are up quite late."

I don't know why she always talks to me this way; she is generally very cold to me, unlike Sarah. She was smirking even now when she added: "Is anything wrong?"

"*Wrong*?" I felt pleasure just thinking of my encounter with Alex, and it gave me even sweeter pleasure than I cared to let on. Hence the word startled me. "Wrong? In what way?"

"With my brother and you . . . of course."

"No," I said. "Nothing is wrong, I assure you."

I walked past her then, feeling very superior, until I was in my room again and the light was on and I was staring at these pages where it was clear that somebody had been in my absence.

Could it have been Perl? Why? For what possible reasons?

I remember going to the window once again and there was now the faintest glimmering of powdery blue rubbed into the horizon with almost painterly care, signifying the approach of morning. In the garden a first thrush warbled. I stared below me into the soft darkness. A pick fell somewhere against the earth . . . once . . . twice . . . thrice . . . its thudding was almost pleasant to hear.

Again I turned to my diary. Why would Perl care to know any of my secrets? What use did she think she could make of them? No. It could not have been Perl. It was either Aunt Ilona or Pepi, or Alex himself.

But it was very bitter for me to think such a thing. I tried to shutter my mind closed to it, but this thought persisted. That Alex has smiled at me because he felt somehow the wiser, having read what I have written here about him.

So there was not even a moment of adulation in his glance. Like his father, it was all a matter of the purest calculation. Somehow he has entered my room and has been through all these pages . . . and when he came he would be sure to be telling me such things. Of that I was certain. He was intending to berate me with what he has learned.

Going to the door of my bedroom, I bolted it closed. I would not admit Alex, even if he did make the effort to come to me. I also bolted the adjacent door into Aunt Pepi's room, for I would have no further intruders of any sort. Again I returned to the window sill. In the distance the horizon was now the palest azure, but, when one looked directly down into the garden, darkness and shadows prevailed everywhere. I had my hands against my face, peering out into the void of this early morning. Again the thought crossed my mind that I might flee this place, but the thought surrendered to its own lassitude and I was shortly dozing, again near sleep.

The first rays of direct sun at morning have awakened me. The fragrant violets are in bloom. Strawberry leaves have begun to show themselves and the little white fragrant lilies which are my namesakes. In the meadow near Kolasz a field of purple bulbs of some sort exploding . . . It is at least seventy-six degrees in the shade. It must soon grow even warmer.

A great commotion downstairs and throughout the town. The sound of construction splits the quiet air. I have dressed rapidly and will shortly be joining the family at the breakfast table, but with the knowledge that somebody has been here, obscenely peering over my shoulder, I must take a moment to pause and consider what is to be done. Since I have no more secrets from these people, they shall be able to keep none from me. From this time, from now on, I shall be on my guard toward everyone. They will not be able to deceive me again. I shall be watching them even when they least expect it.

We have no more than forty-eight hours left in Clig. Like naughty children seeking to avoid punishment, the very thing we all feared has happened . . .

Worse. It is even worse. Without provocation, it has walked over to us brazenly and slapped us hard across the cheek.

So cruel. It is so cruel. The wicked are not punished. *We* are punished. *Every one of us. Mothers. Little children. Old people. Our friends, our neighbors.* Yes, I pity myself but I pity some of them even more. Surely some of them are innocents. Did they receive our assurances? Did they crave after these things as we surely did? What shall it matter to me now when it is all so loathsome to me? Not to speak of our betrayer with his loathsome, haughty ways . . .

How am I to express the cruelty of the way this thing is being done. "There will be no 'exceptions.' " The entire city and its suburbs— "*Judenrein.*" We are herded together like cattle in the principal square. We wait there until it is nearly tea time. *We grumble. We stay. We listen,* and then we are sent home again to pack our belongings, told we have no more than forty-eight hours left to us in Clig. Our destinies have been decided. We shall be sent to work elsewhere, those of us who are lucky.

It has all happened so precipitously that, even now, I tremble to think of what we were told, as if it was just another of my daydreams. Can it be that they will uproot even the aged? Are none to be spared? It is brutal and senseless. Why now, when our liberators must be so close at hand? How do they expect to profit from any of this? We have been irrevocably betrayed, but by whom?

The others are equally shocked. Alex was with me the whole time until we had to depart for medical examinations, but he could say nothing that wasn't obvious. Uncle Newman looks and acts like a dead man. I pity him least of all. Was it not he who sought out all these assurances? He and Alex and my aunt.

Of all I pity most Sarah and Maurice and their child. So little and so harmless, and yet he is just as much an enemy of our wicked state as any of the rest of us. I am reminded of the girl who stood next to me in the sheds when we were being examined. She was only just on the verge of womanhood, with tiny bosoms, and the beginnings of a maternal swelling. What does she have to look forward to now?

From the general commotion in the lower floors of the house it is obvious that plans are being concocted. I can take part in none of this. It is all fruitless and wicked. We are the enemies of Hungary and we will be treated as enemies. Nobody will protest. Our neighbors shall be the accomplices to all this. Before we say adieu to them, the looters will be among us.

I sit in my room behind a barred door with dry pinpricks in my throat and a heaviness in my chest. It is the end. We have no hope. It has all been decided: *"What Destiny has ordained your futures shall be . . ."* I could scream from my heart. Now that the very worst has happened I do not even think of M and my shame. We were told it was the fault of saboteurs in Plevnitz. *If only some of us had their courage . . .* But I think it is not even so, not true about this Plevnitz; it is all just another lie, told to lull us into not taking up arms. They seem to wish us to go wherever it is without a struggle, as if it were in the nature of these humbugs to do anything other.

At the square I did not see my Communist lady, although I am sure that she must be at least part Jew, but I saw Wenckner, who was father's comrade in the Social Democratic Federation. What could he say? Could gentiles protest when men like Uncle Newman merely wound their watches and wrote memoranda to themselves about the state of their affairs?

The Wenckners of this world leave us only their words. Such words! How I remember them. Father orating in French: *"D'une confrontation incessante avec des adversaires puissants, cyniques, et menteurs . . ."*

Bold noble words of defiance and protest addressed to the men of power *"à Paris, à Berlin, à Hambourg, à Francfort, à Londres, à Washington, à Bruxelles, à la Vienne, à Genève, à Oslo, à Le Hague, à Tunis, Alger, Moscou, Budapest, Bombay, Calcutta, New Delhi, Rangoon, Bangkok, Singapour, Hongkong, Manille, Tapei, Tokio; des milliers des kilomètres parcourus de camp en camp, de prison en prison, dans la Russe et dans l'Espagne, l'Italie et les États Unis.*

"Et le monde avait vecu et nous sommes damnés encores . . ."

There is a great commotion in the front hall. Angry voices—". . . *des adversaires puissants, cyniques, et menteurs . . ."* Something is about to happen. I do not wish to know of it, and yet cannot resist eavesdropping. I will go to the landing, to my safety place of shadows, and listen to what is being said. Even if it is only more of the same deceit, I wish to know of it.

I feel ashamed to find myself so reduced to the common acrimony. We are not nice people. Perhaps we deserve our fate? Why? Because we are not so? What of pain, pleasure, terror, joy? These are surely ours despite what we may be. Our spirits—do they quicken the less because we are so rude and selfish and spoiled, yes, and cowardly?

What is human, after all? To be human is to be abject. Surely it is so . . . Now more than ever I wish I could express myself in words. There is a havoc inside me and I wish only to scream.

Write? What is there to write? The infection spreads everywhere. We are a disease. Everything, *all*, is over now. It is almost a relief, as if all the pretenses had been discarded and we faced each other fairly and unashamed, like loving savages.

There are leaving me behind and I tell myself now I don't even care.

What else can I say?

I know who I am and I know who they are. The common acrimony has reduced me to a snail. I cling to the glass of my resentments. I am nothing if not tenacious and resourceful about expressing my resentments. I am certainly no better than the others. Do they know this as I do? Look at them.

I would kill Uncle Newman except that I believe others may be happy to do this for me.

As for Alex, the less said the better . . . He is his mother's son, his parents' child. A good boy, not like all the rest of us selfish ones.

Soon they are going. I am to be left behind. They will not be able to forget me. They will not be able to hide from me. They must not.

I will not be so rude as to say more things, to make more accusations, as I did at the breakfast table today. But I will be there when they are leaving. I will not let them squirm out of my sight. They must be made to know what they are doing with their trading and their secrets behind my back. They have treated me like some kind of thing and I can have no pity on any of them except, perhaps, for Aunt Ilona. She thinks she has lost her little Perl. Now she goes around weeping, helpless, a silly old woman. Let her weep and pretend if it distracts her from the truth.

Concerning little Mr. Stinkfinger himself, my former fiancé, Mr. Shandor Yagodah, perhaps it is good riddance. The less said the better of a person who would do such a thing when I had so much trust in him. I trusted him to be my consoler but he is not even capable of that. If I had married such a cretin, I should have regretted it all my life . . .

All my life! Fancy that I should still wish to cling to such optimistic phrases even now. It is like Skirzeny wishing to have this place back in return for his so-called favors.

But I hear voices. They are moving crates. The wagons have arrived.

Somewhere near Gidelve, mid-summer, 1944:

I am M's whore at last and I do not mind it nearly as much as I mind the awful weather and these continual bombardments, the shellings of the hills far apace, the short rations. We have had nothing but wet, hot stickiness and grey skies for a week.

It isn't exactly pleasant here where we are, although Miklos is a perfect gentleman with me, taking his pleasure like a gentleman; he is perfectly correct in all ways. It appears his Jewess pleases him.

I think often of my father and mother.

They loved me, I think, but they never loved each other. How do I know? Who better than their own child? In addition, my mother once told me something. I think she was preparing to take a lover. "Your father is a tired old man and I am still a young woman. It is very hard for me sometimes."

Poor father! Our little Socialist. He made love to the world with his words and died of a stroke on the eve of being cuckolded.

I loved my father dearly and it has been so very long since I had the chance of thinking of him, or speaking of him. With whom was I to speak? That pig Uncle Newman.

Father managed to die in his sleep, which is more than one can say for the rest of our clan. Fancy them, as Skirzeny insists I know of it, packed in goods trains, and racing to heaven-knows-what destination. How I miss them all, my father, Alex, and Uncle Newman especially. I continually believe that I must and should do something fitting, such as pray for them, but don't know whether it is proper for a girl to pray the *Yisgadal* and I don't even know the actual words of the prayer and so I make up the likely sounds, mix them with certain gentile words, and mumble certain of these to myself with a suitable earnestness. The others must think me mad. Why do I pray? Does Pepi benefit from my prayers? Do I know for certain that she is no longer among the living? I pray for all of them like a crazy hermit because I miss them all so and, angry as I am, I do not hate them.

I miss my father especially, because he used to love me so very very much. He used to say: "You have your mother's face and good looks, of course, but your heart is not so much its own master."

Oh, come back, Father, and let me show you your daughter.

Father, your daughter is the mistress of a gypsy bastard and your family and kinsmen have betrayed me and are now busily betraying each other.

Alone. I am alone, left to pray, who never learned to pray before; even at bedtime, as a fretful child, it was not considered the approved thing for the daughter of my father to make even gentile prayers. But now I pray with perfect cynicism, and rage, and pity. I pray often by myself and listen to the household prayers of these others when they see fit to do such things. Alex, Alex, you fool . . . For the rest, you have no right to judge: I provide a good deal of pleasure, and nobody is the worse for having known me.

Nobody except little Shandor, of course. I was rather cruel to him and so unforgiving. I am still unforgiving. It cannot be helped. We were lovers. It had to be that I would some day feel something. It is just too bad that what I felt was hate and that I had to make him so aware of my feelings.

That day before he left when we said those things to each other, Alex said to me: "I have always loved you, Lilo."

And to his father, he cried: "Let me be a man for once in my life."

He said he wished to stay behind. It tore my heart to hear him say those things because it so happened I believed him. I believed in his intentions.

Perhaps if he had not said anything. How much more I could have believed if he had acted and said nothing. But, you see, by speaking out, by crying out, he wished to place the guilt for his inaction at my doorstep whereas I was silent and could blame only him.

How much better if we had acted together . . .

I continue to think of Alex.

That day in the garden he meant to act, I know he did. He meant to speak up because he was really quite a bold person.

He meant to act.

Alex labored over me with a truly protean zeal, I'm afraid, because you see he had to do these things even though he was utterly incapable of feeling anything except that he was proving something to himself.

Because he enjoyed nothing at all.

But with M it is effortless and cruel, like breathing heavily after a long run.

Alex, I don't hate you or blame you or resent you and I know you were not a coward that day in the forest with M and I know you loved your father and I respected you for that, as I loved my father, too.

I could never hate you, Cousin, but I am not the Lilo you knew.

And my life in this household is not at all like what it was in those days. I sometimes felt in that household that everybody was writing entries in a diary about everybody else. A mansion full of snoops and gossips. Everybody a Saint Simonist. The whole household honeycombed with intrigues and within every top drawer of every secretaire a small notebook and pencil, a snatch of prose, opened to the date . . .

Here it is not like that. The life of the Skirzenies is cold commercial transactions, utterly without our self-consciousness. This is a house of rough, ugly dealings, a hearty perversity. Here nobody even pretends to be high-minded. But, then, they don't go trading one another like heifers. The daughters scrap among themselves over clothing and beads. They treat me as their skivvy. They know how frightened I am. And they have so many old resentments to even out . . .

The old man Farnas is here only one or two

nights during the week. His wife reigns over the house like a blackened crone. I have heard gossip that there is another woman somewhere, but I daren't ask. With Miklos I talk only of his pleasure, like a whore.

I am so terribly frightened. I don't pray for myself. I am too frightened. I am all alone here. I have the worst taste in my mouth all the time. I keep remembering Alex as he peered out at me through the wagon that day. The day he left. He hated me just as I hated him. And he had tried to act, I know he did, and yet I blamed only him . . .

I think I shall not be writing in this diary for a little while. What if it were found? They would think that I was planning to betray them too. Tonight I shall be alone (for Miklos has gone off with his father to make the final arrangements about reoccupying the Yagodah house) and I shall pretend to be asleep when he comes home. He will know that it is a pretense. I know he will. *Tant pis!* I must try to think about running away . . .

Yagodah house, Clig:

We have occupied the house again. Skirzeny says he is going to make an apartment for Miklos and me in the cellar. Cousins from somewhere east have arrived. The whole establishment is in an uproar.

I must try to think about running away.

I am living on soda water biscuits and margarine and tea. I lose weight. I can't eat their food. M is attentive. Yesterday he picked berries for me, but they were so tart and sweet that they hurt my gums.

Things to do: Think about running away . . .

When I look in the mirror I see a girl with badly chapped lips. For the past week a small sore has been forming on the smooth skin above my left eye. I don't think I look very beautiful.

Suppose I were to lose my looks?

＊

Suppose I am to lose my looks?

This wet heat continues. My skin feels all mildewed.

The Yagodahs have perished.

Skirzeny tells me this and that Councilor Ujlaki also came to visit and Farnas made him confirm the thing.

I wander about the house saying prayers in nonsense syllables.

Hear O Israel

I am with dysentery, cramps, and watery stools.

＊

There has been a massacre of Jewish girls nearby. They were hiding out in the woods and they were discovered. I have overheard the whole story. It happened the very day of the resettlement.

Miklos pretends not to feel anything about what has happened, but tonight he was very loving to me. And he has seemed so listless and disinterested of late, I thought, perhaps, because of all the heat . . .

M is increasingly loving to me. He no longer does what he used to do. He kisses me and wishes that I kiss him too. I do it and I lose myself in the act.

The heat has lifted momentarily.

M has grown very good to look at. He has had his hair cut. He is growing a blonde mustache. In the mornings I love to see the tight hairs along his lean young body flash against the sunlight when he dresses. One of his sisters, I believe, is jealous of me. Today she said: "If you have a little bastard you'll have to answer for it."

The old woman doesn't speak to me. The cousins get drunk early in the day and sprawl about the sitting rooms downstairs, muttering obscenities. They worry about the end of the war, their properties in Dobruja, and curse

Xanthos, the local bank president, for freezing certain assets. Skirzeny, however, remains calm and perversely good-humored. He calls me "daughter" with a lewd grin.

It is believed that there are advance detachments of the "liberating forces" less than twenty kilometres away.

※

My head and stomach ache now all the time.

M is cold again. I am indolent. The daughters are busy packing every possession of the Yagodahs into large wooden barrels. I hide in the cellar, where we used to store my parents' things, and I feed bits of soda water cracker to the mice.

Miklos calls me "the little Saxon," or "my little Saxoness," or "my woman."

His father laughs and makes a filthy noise like retching.

More than what Miklos has ever done to me, he humiliates . . . But there was once a time when M called me "love" and, once, in his sleep, "my own."

Supposing I am losing my looks.

I go around in rags, no energy to dress. And, of course, I am not allowed to roam outside alone.

We are going on an excursion tomorrow to visit other relatives. But I am feeling so very weak. I wish I didn't have to go. How can I think about running away when there are all those dead animals in the fields . . .

Do I take care of myself? How? Why? What is to be gained for me now?

The old woman says she wishes for a grandson. I have taken no precautions but I do not seem able to conceive. Perhaps it is my "condition" or perhaps I am too undernourished.

M is going away. He says it will only be a matter of weeks. I am to stay with his father and the rest of the family in the woods. The old house is to be locked up once again. I debate whether to take my diary with me.

Our departure is delayed another day. Today Skirzeny brought me some dresses and skirts he said were taken from a wealthy Jewish family. They are the kind of gaudy things that streetwalkers and the girls in houses wear. I refuse to accept them. He grins, and then he asks his daughter to lend me a *dirndl* and apron and I am to wear a kerchief tied around my head at all times like Magda, our cook.

I walk about the house
I cry without provocation

I don't seem to be able to help myself

Miklos sees me and it makes him very upset.

I can tell

But I am always so very hungry here and I have these cramps . . .

My face is all broken out.

It never used to happen to me. I try to wash the pores in soap and water but the terrible red blotches remain.

My skin hurts too, even when I smile.

Alex and I were always trying to be good to each other. We cared so much about hurting the other's feelings that we were betrayers and murderers.

Without a doubt I am as guilty as the rest. I needed sin. I needed pain. I needed . . .

Hunger
Hunger
Hunger
Death. Nothing is simpler. But this is murder.

Hear O Israel
O God, why hast thou forsaken me?

A number of Hungarians are being rounded up. Nobody seems to know why. What have they done? Again nobody seems to know. There is an air of mystery everywhere. Lips are sealed. God, how they did not count on this.

With grim solemnity I have a visitor, Farnas Skirzeny.

"It appears my son is bewitched. For his own sake I shall not allow this to happen.

"True, you may say, a man who despises his own son is hardly the one to be so protective— and in times like these. He is our first-born. Did you think we were any less proud than you Jews about these matters?

"I have risked much for you and your family. You think I betrayed *them*, but they betrayed themselves. They were so blind. But now I must demand from you cooperation.

"Miklos is to go away on a 'business trip.'

"You will remain here with us, under my protection. In fact, you will be our safe-conduct whereas Miklos has been so 'political' that he can no longer afford you . . .

"I don't expect you to understand. Bear in mind, nothing you will do can stop this. Do you understand me?"

I am dumbstruck. I nod dumbly.

Skirzeny: "Yid bitch, don't pretend not to understand!"

Later Miklos comes. Nothing is said. He doesn't want me, I can tell that, but we must do it even so. When we are supposed to be drowsing, I think I can hear him weeping. Early in the morning he rises like a black cloud, is gone.

He has left behind this note:

> I hate you. I never wish to see
> you again. Jew whore, what do
> you think you know of me?
> Why are you staring at me all the
> time. You stare and stare. Why?
> You are filthy, ugly, and you
> always smell bad. You wretched
> thing, why should I wish to see
> you ever again? You are a whore.
> You are disgusting to me. Cunt!
> Sow! I don't wish to see you
> again. M

Now I am truly all alone.

Again I pray nonsense to a nonsense God . . .

Hear O Israel

Lord God, why have you forsaken me?

Lord God of our fathers, why have you forsaken?

Alex Alex the Lord thy God who am I?

Dear God, Dear Murderer, thy will be done

Thy Kingdom come
Our Father, Our King
Give us this day our Daily Hunger
Our Father which art in Heaven
Curse us, despise us, murder us, betray us
O Lord Our God Thou hast set up a table
before us
In the presense of our enemies
My cup runneth over . . .

I have terrible bleeding sores inside my
mouth . . . and wish I could remember the
words of the *Yisgadal* . . . *V'Yisgadal* . . .
V'yisroman . . . But my lips are always so
chapped and I have these sores . . .

Herr Gott!

Endlich begann's . . . *mir standen lang am
Fenster in dieser Woch* . . . *ein Tag nach dem
andern* . . . *immer ein Nachtmittag* . . . *mir
standen am Fenster* . . . *my cup runneth over
. . . lange Zeit gegenüber dem alten Kastanien-
baum* . . . *lange Zeit* . . . *in dieser Woch immer
am Nachtmittag* . . . *lange Zeit.* . . .

Afterword

One writes to enter other lives; to invent lives that one can hope to enter into.

The precious stuff of a life begins to reveal itself in the sullen face of a black orphan; or, even, the lies of the middle-class careerist.

To write a novel, then, is an act of complicity and exculpation.

But one novel ends and another begins; there is then supposed to intervene the rule of the clean slate. One constructs, after all, only fictions . . .

Thus the dead are shoveled under, and one is enjoined to invent new sufferers.

How?

Why?

Men are often haunted by spirits about whom they must invent memories. My contemporaries are the dead children of Europe past and Asia present.

R. M. Elman
Vermont
December 6, 1967

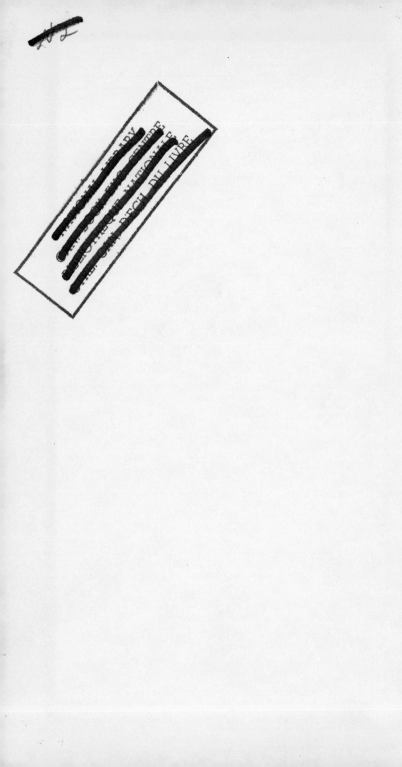